Green
A *Blue Feet* Anthology

green

A *Blue Feet* Anthology

Anneliese Abela * Aden Burg * Chloe Cannell
Dante DeBono * Lyndal Hordacre Kobayashi
Evan Jarrett * Belinda Lees
Heather Briony McGinn * Lily Roberts
Eugene Tabios * Simon-Peter Telford

Edited by Alex Dunkin

Buon-Cattivi Press
Adelaide, Australia

Contents

EDITOR'S NOTES AND ACKNOWLEDGEMENTS

by Dr Alex Dunkin

Green: A Blue Feet Anthology draws upon the hidden gems of creative researchers. This collection of verse and prose represents candidates currently undertaking higher degrees by research and who are part of the Critical Creative Reading and Writing Collective (CCRWC). Contributors were asked to respond to the theme of 'green' and they did so through an extensive array of creative answers. The authors' works challenge and embrace the world around them and their unique personal experiences. It is from these writings that we can read the complexities and accomplishments of the next wave of creative writers undertaking academic research to underpin their knowledge and demonstrated talent.

Creative pieces from eleven authors were selected for *Green: A Blue Feet Anthology*. The chosen submissions complement and speak to each other in the longer narrative of the anthology, which explores and expresses the cornucopia of the natural and lived world around us. They intertwine and echo back to each other in a manner where individual creativity becomes a conversation among peers who are in their early steps of grounding themselves in the overlapping realms of academia and creative industries. The texts explore the full extent of lifecycles, scaling the early stages of discovery and passion, and leading to the reflections that arise when arriving at an end. It is in this full lifecycle narrative that this anthology has been structured, including the experimental diversions and intermissions that might arise. While the full narrative is styled to be read as one complete collection, each piece can be snatched out as a standalone performance to be enjoyed as desired in a particular moment.

Green: A Blue Feet Anthology was initiated and produced on the traditional lands of the Kaurna people. We respect their spiritual relationship with their country. We acknowledge the Kaurna people as the custodians of the Adelaide region and that their cultural and heritage beliefs are still as important to the living Kaurna people today.

This work was supported in part by the University of South Australia. Proceeds from sales of this anthology go to Trees For Life Inc.

Foreword

by Dr Jessica White

The word 'green' stems from the Old English word *grēne*, which is of Germanic origin, and is related to the words 'grass' and 'grow'. The life cycle of grass is marked by its growth from seed to seedling, to flowering, to senescence and to death. *Green: A Blue Feet Anthology* is shaped by a similar life cycle, gathering poetry and prose through stages of beginning, unfurling, expanding and concluding. It indicates how, whether we are conscious of it or not, the natural world infuses our writing.

The theme of time influences not only the structure of this collection, but also many of its pieces. Anneliese Abela's 'Sentient Beings' dwells upon the progression of seasons on a farm. She uses sensory detail, particularly sound and smell, to evoke the drama of animal lives, a refreshing shift from human-centred narratives. Eugene Tabios also charts the passing of time through intense focus on a café and its customers, an apt series of vignettes given how much some writers like their coffee. With rich and compact prose, Heather McGinn reaches back into the past to recount a life with grandparents. The rhythm of her writing evokes the simple and nourishing routines of tea, scones and mending. Chloe Cannell's 'Emerald or Teal Green?' is full of colour, fabric, love and tension. Charting the push and pull of relationships, she shows the reader that friendship and love have a life cycle too, one that can make itself known in unexpected ways. Evan Jarrett's 'Green Beach' experiments with time, compelling his protagonist to understand that external forces such as the sea pay no mind to human temporality. On a different scale, Dr Amelia Walker moves into a grub's world, bringing aeons of evolution into the present with the bite of a leaf.

In a collection based on growth, plants and other living things feature prominently, Lily Roberts' work blends the sensual and quotidian. With her nets of poetry she captures stars, pomegranate seeds, rain, cocoons, butterflies and cherries to reflect the fragility and strength of the self. Lyndal Hordacre Kobayashi plays with senses, perception and typology to prompt the reader to consider a blend of image and word. Dante DeBono's poems chart the sheer joy of a plant obsession. She describes chlorophyllous companionship during Covid-19 lockdowns and stretches back into deep time to contemplate the growth of bacteria and oxygen that led to the greening of the world. She considers the future too, evoking the cultural and personal anxiety associated with smashed avocados and finances. Belinda Lees' character in 'If Only Fences Kept Us Apart' is similarly fretful about affording and managing a house. In an entertaining account of what happens when one's faith in recycling is not shared by others, she charts the flow of money and power in the real estate ecosystem. Meanwhile, growth occurs not only in plants stretching to the light, but also through the psyche, as Aden Burg describes in 'Fresh Inspiration', an account of a boy and an older man playing a game of Shogi.

In the final section, Simon-Peter Telford's 'What if I Called You Wally?', a whale and an elderly man, adrift from their pods at the end of their lives, sit upon a shore. The protagonist realises the futility of helping the whale, wounded and beached. The story is a reminder that what grows must always decay, and evokes the spectre of extinction hovering over so many plants, animals and invertebrates in the Anthropocene. This collection writes back against the disregard for nonhuman life by centring it in creative and original ways.

Green: A Blue Feet Anthology is also about growing writers. Publication is a key aspect of building a profile as a writer, and the editor, Dr Alex Dunkin, is to be commended for overseeing this collection, and for nurturing a new generation of thoughtful and exciting writers.

Creative Introduction

by Dr Amelia Walker

Situation: critical. That's my most to-the-point account of life on Earth right now. I use the word *critical* as it is used in hospital and emergency settings: a critical condition, wherein miniscule decisions bear life versus death significance; a situation of importance, demanding the careful attention and attentive care Donna Haraway calls response-ability.[1] *Situation: critical* rings in my mind and quickens my heart every time there's news of raging bushfires, quenching tsunamis, earthquakes, and extinction, or equally, of insidious 'slow violences' like soft plastics, air pollution, reckless mining, unsustainable farming, and more.[2] *Situation: critical* describes ever-escalating warfare, shootings, starvation, dispossession, tyranny, and the violent injustices of privilege versus oppression. *Situation: critical* neatly sums up the dominant culture here in Australia, as in the United States and elsewhere: racism, homophobia, transphobia, ableism, xenophobia, and countless other varieties of needless hate

---

1 Haraway, D 2012 'Awash in Urine: DES and Premarin® in Multispecies Response-ability', *Women's Studies Quarterly*, vol. 40, no. 1/2, pp. 301-316.
2 Nixon, R 2011 *Slow Violence and the Environmentalism of the Poor*, Harvard University Press, Cambridge, MA.

and discrimination perpetrated daily by people who could just as easily practice kindness.

Situation: critical. Undoubtedly. How can we respond?

Grim as things might be, the word *critical* is, to me, also positively laden. In life-or-death scenarios, life remains on the cards. Action still matters. Arguably, it matters more: this might be the ultimate chance. As Raymond Williams noted in *Keywords* (1976), criticality is linked with *crisis*, which in turn bears the notion of a crossroads or turning point: a chance to change behaviour, to pursue a different path.[3] Any considered response to the critical therefore must, I argue, engage creativity, which following Williams requires acts of original thinking that consider things in new, innovative ways to identify possibilities that could otherwise remain ignored.[4] Arts practices including writing, sketching, painting, music, and movement provide ways to pursue and share creative thinking. That is why I believe the arts matter so much right now, in education, research, and society broadly.

The Critically Creative Reading and Writing Collective (CCRWC) is a community and a space for people to connect and pursue creative thinking about critical issues in a university-based context of research and teaching. In academia, the word *critical* bears additional implications atop those I have already noted. Criticism in the sense of literary criticism, cultural criticism and/or critique suggests thinking and writing wherein theory, rigor, and acts of judgement reign supreme.[5] Unfortunately, this view of criticality sometimes places it in opposition to the creative, which suffers discredit

---

3 Williams, R 1976 [2015] *Keywords: A Vocabulary of Culture and Society*, Oxford, New York, p. 47.

4 Williams, R 1976 [2015] Keywords: A vocabulary of Culture and Society, Oxford, New York, pp. 46-47.

5 See reference in endnote three.

for its purportedly over-subjective, haphazard elements. This critical/creative split is associated with others including that of theory from practice, logic from affect, and experiential knowing from so-called evidence-based fact, all of which are in turn elements of a 'two cultures' dichotomy that dates from the early twentieth century at least, which Williams unsettled by showing criticism to be more than judgement in the sense of fault-finding.[6]

Despite strong cases from Williams, among others, the creative/critical split persists. The CCRWC's name strategically connects them, signalling our refusal to extricate theory from practice, experience from evidence, emotion from logic, or artistic imagination from scholarly rigor. To be critically creative is to pursue praxis enhanced by reciprocities between the arts, research, and thinking via all imaginable senses. The CCRWC looks to and learns from 'creative critical' writing and 'craft-criticism'.[7] Our group is, however, to my knowledge unique in our structure and processes. We are a reading group who meet monthly to collaboratively unpack a scholarly article relevant to creative practice and/or arts research, but for us, the unpacking crucially includes activities such as writing or sketching in response to reading-inspired prompts. The imaginative processes of producing and sharing creative work enrich our explorations into complex ideas. We thereby broach an extended range of possibilities for applying new ideas in and to arts practices and/as arts-based inquiry.

The works in this anthology grew from CCRWC workshop

---

6 For 'the two cultures', see Snow, CP 1959 [1998] *The Two Cultures*, Cambridge University Press, Cambridge, UK. For criticism as fault finding, see endnote three.

7 For 'creative-critical', see Hilevaara, K & Orley, E 2018 The Creative Critic: Writing as/about Practice, Routledge, Oxon. For 'craft-criticism', see Adsit, J 2018 Critical Creative Writing: Essential Readings on the Writer's Craft, Bloomsbury Academic, London.

prompts themed around the colour green, in connection with readings relating to the Anthropocene.[8] The dialogues we shared at these intensives centred around questions of how artists, writers and thinkers can best contribute to the social conversations and actions the Anthropocene demands—or, to recall Haraway once more, how we can enact creative response-ability.[9] The diverse pieces this book collects reflect those dialogues and our differing-though-connected ways of thinking through the intense issues and questions at hand. Each contribution, in its own way, attending its own focus, recognises and reminds, the situation is indeed critical. This is our creative response.

8 The Anthropocene refers to climate change, pollution, extinction, and multiform other problems that bring us to crisis today. See Tandon, SK 2021 'The Anthropocene Concept', *Journal of the Geological Society of India*, vol. 97, no. 1, pp. 563-566.
9 Refer to footnote one.

*what begins and
continues to cycle*

eorðe
by Dante DeBono

Picture it.
Endless darkness, the quiet of solitude.
A rock floating through the newly expanded universe,
the bare surface shifting to establish its atmosphere,
to create its glassy oceans.
Colonies of amorphous bacteria forming,
spreading in layers, waves,
pouring out of those that came before,
self-replicating to create patterns
that span the length of the planet
like the sliced core of a malachite crystal.
Micro-monsters populate the water,
no need for eyes as there's nothing yet to see,
just to be felt through their single-celled forms,
the encompassing comfort of water all they will know.
They merely exist, unphased by their sparse surroundings,
drifting for millennia before evolving once more.
Time passes, gradually, but it's picking up speed.
The creatures crawl out from the depths,
breathing in virgin air as they turn to the sun,
making their homes on continental crusts,
clear open lands that one day,
in the distant future,
will be green with boundless life.

Life cycle
by Dante DeBono

beneath the soil,
the seed is hidden, buried,
biding time to grow

sprouting olive trees,
to passersby, look like weeds,
praying to survive

if you are patient
your tree will age and bear fruit
to share with others

small and private child
steps inside a mirrored world
where every surface calls her by her name

intricate patterns on the carpet
curtains waving at me like a sad old friend
anchovies in the salsa verde
wet and oily on my toast, my buttered skin

all the world contained
inside a tear drop
the bones of last year's animals dug up
from the garden

the camera catches him watching old movies
it catches us kiss, it catches us choose

seeds push matter out of themselves
and punnets become plastic houses of worship
spread out before me in the sunshine
ever quiet

souls of the graveyard cast a rainbow
its colours dance along the water's veil
garden grows, a living chapel
and me, the child, at its centre:
performing surgery after the resurrection

(backyard homily)
by Lily Roberts

Precious
by Dante DeBono

He holds out two hands,
        and resting in each of his weathered palms
                is a stone.

'One,' he says, 'is an emerald.
        It has been in our family for generations.
                The other
        is merely a piece of sea glass,
                smoothed by the waves of the ocean.'

The child looks,
        studies both the small, green rocks,
                crystalline and glowing with refracted
                sunlight.

'Which is which?' the old man asks.

        The child replies, 'I don't know.'
                And the man smiles, nods.

'Because the only difference between the two
                is judgement.'

Sentient Beings
by Anneliese Abela

Autumn winds drift up from the creek bed below, whistling over the hills to shake the branches of gum and olive trees. It bends the lopsided wooden pickets of paddock fences and rattles the wire coils. Raindrops fall from the edge of corrugated iron roofs to soak the earth, dark and soft after last night's storm. The clouds settle in, morning fog creeping closer across the valley. A trio of kookaburras perches in the tallest eucalypt, their cacophony of laughter echoing through the skies. There is still more rain to come.

Glimpses of sunlight peek through rusted cracks of weathered coops, waking everyone in their sawdust beds. The geese rise first and begin to bellow, their sharp honks alerting the rest of the animals to the start of a new day. The ducks wait just inside the entrance of their houses, a row of old hutches with handmade, creaking chain-link doors. The ducks fold their webbed feet over the edge and jump out onto the sodden earth below. Black and white Muscovy erupt in their excitable squeaks, tail feathers wagging as they waddle over to greet neighbours after their overnight separation. A red-billed drake chases a female around the back of the wheat barrels, hissing at her as his sharp-clawed feet slap at the ground. The sound of wheat berries pouring into his breakfast dish distracts him long enough for the small duck to get away and rejoin the other girls grouping around an old algae-stained bathtub. They drink together, their bills blowing bubbles on the surface of the water.

Two tiny Pekins, their bodies a snowy white, huddle at the back of their box, pressed together while the other ducks waddle out to the paddock. The smaller Pekin's eyes are a clouded, milky grey, her vision vanishing with each passing day, but her friend remains by her side and guides her slowly to their makeshift pond that is brimming with fresh water for their morning swim. The two quiet girls glide across the water as the morning sun warms their feathered backs, their orange legs paddling lazily beneath the surface. Twelve geese exit their house in single file, screaming as the fresh air hits their faces. They rush down the trodden path towards the open field and stretch their wings wide to pluck at newly sprouted grass blades emerging from the dirt.

The smell of lanolin hits the air as four sheep rush uphill through the dense fog, alerted by the screaming geese. Their wool is damp to the touch, but the thick layer keeps their bodies warm and dry. The youngest of the flock, a hand-raised ewe, leads the girls through the empty field. She is two years old, her dark eyes bright as stars, her nose a soft pink, and she remembers distant days spent inside the old weatherboard house atop the hill. Her cloven hooves tapped the floorboards as she skipped around on lanky legs, chasing after the cats and house dogs. She suckled milk through a bottle beside the heat of crackling embers. And before that—stumbling across an empty road, crying out for her lost mother, driven away from her in a black cloud of choking haze, wandering aimlessly with a broken heart and an empty stomach—she was scooped up, swaddled in rags, and brought to the old house.

She leads the three other sheep towards the fresh pile of cereal set down for them inside their paddock gate. It counts as second breakfast, for they've already spent an hour or two down the valley, grazing on whip thistle and fleabane, the prickly weeds presently numbing their lips and gums. In the next paddock over, a sixteen-year-old goat with a Billy Gruff beard limps on arthritis-stricken front legs. He looks up with an indignant bleat as a pile of fruit is placed on the ground beside him. Bending his wobbly legs, he rests on his knees to examine the assortment. He sniffs at the leafy celery stalks before picking up a black overripe banana and squishing it—peel and all—between his teeth. His gristly beard swings beneath his chin as he chews. The rectangular pupils in his golden eyes watch as rain clouds drift closer, and he turns to look back longingly at his enclosed shelter. He will not linger over a leisurely breakfast today, keen to return to his warm, dry straw bed.

Light floods into the hay shed as the heavy door is unlatched. A gust of valley wind forces the door to swing backward and slam against the red-painted wall. The bang of metal startles the horses and ponies nearby, sending a flight of wild pigeons into the air from an overhanging gum tree. The pigeons' satin bodies move in a flailing attempt of synchronised rhythm as they circle overhead and then settle back down into the still-rustling branches. A small tabby yawns and jumps down from the hay bales in the shed, rubbing her body against the rough edges of straw. Her gaze lingers on the tin of cat biscuits atop an old wine barrel. The pair of chestnut horses hear the tearing of hay and pace keenly up and down their pens, snorting loudly. They shake rain from their manes, revealing the freeze band identification markings on their necks from distant days of racing. The gentle giants still race one another to breakfast, but the rest of the day is spent in well-deserved retirement, the entire property theirs to explore as they wish. Five ponies await their own hay and offerings of carrot and apple, whinnying with impatient delight. The oldest whips his flaxen hair out of his eyes as he curls his lips and reaches out to take delicate bites of apple with long yellow teeth.

The chickens dart across their tall-fenced yard to hide beneath twisting trees, kicking at the damp earth and nestling amongst the leaves, sheltered from the rain and hidden from the piercing eyes of foxes waiting just outside the property. Bubbles rise to the surface of the tortoise pond, and glassy bead-like eyes peek out between water reeds to locate floating pellets of food. Aviary doors swing open and birdseed is scattered, the sound coaxing snuggling doves from their egg boxes and friendly galahs from their perches, pink and grey heads bobbing. Stretching out their toes, they sift through the mix, plucking striped sunflower seeds and cracking open their shells with curved beaks. A bonded pair of rainbow lorikeets splash one another in their birdbath, wolf-whistling and washing remnants of sticky nectar from their faces.

The flock of cooing pigeons, having watched the morning's scene play out from their position in the trees, glide down to sneak into breakfast dishes and finish off any leftover crumbs. A young magpie hops across fence pickets, looking for a lone crust of bread somehow missed by the still-honking geese. An ostentation of majestic peafowl struts across the driveway, brown females crouching low as the males spread their full tails and preen at them, emerald feathers rustling with a metallic shimmer. One of the peahens moves cautiously in the shadows of winding leafy vines, four tiny peachicks darting after her, their infant bodies covered in a fluffy down. In the treetops above, a shining black crow follows their every move, watching the babies with his determined midnight eyes.

The day rolls on and the swirls of fog vanish from the hills, leaving clear, crisp air filled with petrichor. The geese line up at the claw-foot tub, honking impatiently as they await their turn to swim. One by one, they climb in and bow their heads beneath the water, droplets rolling off their backs the minute they resurface. The ducks huddle beneath the flowering trumpet vine and sleep the day away under an awning of pink blossoms. At the departure of rain clouds, the old goat stretches his stiff joints to venture back outside, letting the sun warm his belly and tired bones. The horses and sheep disappear down the valley, not to be seen again until sunset.

And when the sun does dip low beyond the hills, the animals gather again at their pens and hutches for their supper, voices soft and eyelids heavy after another day. Doors and gates creak open and everyone climbs into soft beds. There is a rustle of straw as a family of mice scurries back underground through holes in the duck house floor. The chickens perch on the rungs of an old wooden ladder. The horses and ponies are shut safely in their stables. Four bleating sheep run back uphill, pausing for a quick bite of alfalfa hay and a chin scratch before following one another into their paddock, gate latching behind them. Pigeons and peafowl roost atop sheds and in treetops—the mother peahen digs a nest in the undergrowth and shelters her four chicks beneath her. A plump ginger cat follows the tabby through the hole in the hay shed door and the pair curl up together amongst the bales.

Not every day is the same. Much like the shifting seasons that alter the air and the earth, the lives of the animals bend and change at nature's will. Autumn's chill grows colder and the chicken coop opens to reveal nothing but a mess of feathers, a corner of the tall fence plied away from its frame by fox teeth. Winter winds creep in and silence drifts from the lorikeets' aviary, the surface of their birdbath undisturbed. A soft weeping calls from their nesting log, where one of the pair lays rigid and still, her feet sticking up in the air. Her mate sits close to her and cries out as he presses his head to her rainbow chest. She does not respond. Eighteen years they've spent together. Outside the aviary, the mother peahen guides her offspring beneath the same sheltering vines, but only two of her chirping chicks still follow along, the black crow nowhere to be seen.

It's a bleak midwinter morning and the dark predawn air

is filled with the ominous echo of growling—an unfamiliar sound. Two strange, muscular dogs, lost and far from home, have wandered onto the property overnight. They sit in the sheep paddock. All four ewes lay, broken and scattered across the ground, their throats ripped and wool-covered bodies soaked red, the light gone from their brown eyes. The youngest still stirs, her pink nose twitching until, at last, the stars leave her eyes. She is reunited with her lost mother once more. The dogs guard their kill, but whimper for praise as the paddock gate swings open, their long black tails wagging, no perception of any wrongdoing—they have simply done what dogs do. The old goat trembles in the next pen over, the ducks and geese staring out silently from the safety of their locked huts. The horses kick at the ground, nostrils flared and eyeballs bulging. They all experience the same fear, understand the same pain, understand death.

Despite the darkness and the sorrow, dawn breaks. Light floods the valley and ignites the green hills as it always has, and life goes on. Breakfast is served and hutch doors are opened. A hole is dug, wide and deep, in an empty field. Handfuls of wildflower seeds are sown into the earth above the buried bodies. One final scratch on their soft, crimson-stained chins. The blind Pekin is nervous to leave her box, confused by the snarling and cries that filled the night, terrified of all she cannot see. But her friend is patient and sits by her side until she is ready to emerge, trusting her companion to guide her through the wide, unknown world. By midday, they are swimming together in the pond, tails wagging at the weightless freedom of the water. The old goat is spoiled with three black bananas and snapped branches of olive that he chews on contently. The hay is torn up and shared amongst the ponies. Carrot sticks are crunched in half by long yellow teeth. The mourning lorikeet sits quietly on the edge of his birdbath, reluctantly licking at his nectar. He gives a half-hearted whistle, but still no response.

Spring rolls in, welcome and overdue, with cleansing rain and warming sunshine. New buds sprout on forgotten branches. The fields are covered in lush undergrowth and fresh feed. Whip thistle and fleabane weeds take over, with no sheep left to graze. The two peachicks grow and leap high to follow their mother to the safety of higher roosts. The Muscovy ducks take turns to warm the fragile eggs nestled at the back of their huts. The chicken coop is still empty. Hungry foxes lie in wait. The hay shed door swings open to reveal the graceful tabby burrowed within a hollowed bale of hay. The hay shed fills with soft meows of tiny ginger kittens. Eyes still closed, they crawl over one another as they sniff their way towards their mother's milk.

Buzzing bees hover amongst the trumpet vine, while ducks rest beneath its shade. The lorikeet dampens his beak, and preens his wings as his mate once did, but something catches his attention—the shrieking of birds flying overhead. His feathers puff and he turns his head to the bright blue sky, to the song of wild lorikeets in the treetops above. His voice grows and he sings through his grief with them. Chestnut horses race one another downhill to the creek bed. The geese exit their house in single file, marching through the open field, and bellow as morning sun hits their long necks. They weave through a patch of thriving wildflowers and search for bugs in the fertile earth, their honks alerting everyone to the start of a new day.

Emerald or Teal Green?
by Chloe Cannell

She pulls her hand away from clutching herself to shield from the breeze. She feels a tug and release, her bracelet caught on her green dress. Her breath catches in her throat and she calms herself.

'It's just a thread. It's just a thread,' she repeats in her mind. But it's not just one thread. There's another and it's made a line across her dress. Two lines. The bracelet made her feel fancy because she bought it in Italy on her first and only trip overseas. It was only from a lucky dip so the most expensive thing about it was the flight home, but it reminds her that she could earn her own money to support the things she wanted.

'Makala?' Ash notices her fiddling with her bracelet.

'It caught.' She frowns.

He sidles beside her and brushes her pale pink shoulder while she unclasps the bracelet. She shoves it in her full, rose gold purse. She shakes her head down for a moment—her orange, over-sprayed curls trying to block her view—then looks up with a small smile at the others.

'Anyone need mints? Band Aids? Tissues? I got it,' Makala says.

'I'll take some mints,' Daphne replies from the bench without looking away from her phone, posing with a cartoon dog filter on Snapchat.

Makala rolls her eyes to herself as she passes Daphne some mints. She couldn't imagine being so casual with adults when she was fifteen, but she didn't grow up with siblings in their twenties.

Makala offers them to Barrow, and he waves them away,

straightening his shoulders back while standing next to Ash. His stocky build makes him appear short compared to his tall and athletic younger brother Ash. They are only a couple years apart, but Barrow's hairline is showing the stress of his quarter-life crisis from struggling to find a course or job he wants to see through.

Car tyres crunch against the gravel path. The people in the car look at them for a moment while they glance around the property. They're the only people dressed up, standing beside a bench with the toilets behind them. The car circles at the end of the path, where hedges are waist high, and returns down the driveway.

'Made the same mistake we did. Confusing place, aye?' Barrow says.

'Yeah, I swear Renee talked about this venue more than Craig,' Ash says.

'Her soulmate.' Barrow clasps his hands together across his chest and pops his foot.

Daphne looks up from her phone and glowers at Barrow mockingly.

'Jeez, you look just like Renee when you do that.' Barrow steps back, raising his hands in the air in defence.

Daphne smiles smugly before returning her face to her phone.

'Craig seems good for Renee and I am happy for them, but I'll be glad to not think about this wedding again.' Ash sighs, pushing his fingers through his gelled, dark hair.

'Hey, you promised you'd be into it on the day. I haven't been to a wedding before.' Makala lightly bumps Ash with her shoulder.

He smirks and reaches for his chest as if he's hurt.

'Got to keep the missus happy, unless you don't plan on having a missus like me,' Barrow chuckles. Barrow would be more comfortable pulling a prank in a mankini than a formal suit.

'My first wedding was Mum marrying Jo.' Daphne smiles, her deep berry lipstick bold against her olive complexion.

'Remember when you fainted when Mum was saying "I do" to Soph?' Barrow laughs at Ash, placing his hands on his belly.

Ash rolls his eyes.

There's a big atrium separating the lanes of the gravel driveway, and miles of vines beyond it. The sky is so bright with no buildings in view, but there are some clouds making Makala shiver.

'A blended family wedding sounds beautiful.' Makala moves towards the sunlight while the men complain about their suits being hot under the shelter of the trees. Makala feels one of her false eyelashes droop. She opens the camera on her phone to check while grabbing lash glue out of her purse. She fiddles for a minute, huffs, and gives in. She looks nice. Ignoring the bargain dress and the loose lash, she looks like a wedding guest.

'Vrrrrr,' Makala's phone loudly vibrates. It reads, 'Mum.' She grips the phone quickly to quieten it. Ash reaches out for her hand and squeezes it tight, while Daphne and Barrow are distracted by guests rounding the corner of the nature strip on foot who stop to take pictures by the floral archway.

A man in a white shirt and cowboy hat waves for them to come over from the garden to the hedges.

'Finally.' Barrow waves back.

'Let's get on with it,' Ash mutters.

Makala checks her short nude heels are secure while Barrow and Ash skip down the three short stone steps to the gravel driveway. Daphne jumps the edge of the nature strip in her new, white canvas sneakers. Barrow, Ash, and Daphne are just shy of the hedges when Ash looks back to see Makala wobbling on the gravel driveway. A few other guests appear from the archway photo spot to walk towards the ceremony. They wear mid-length dresses in different colours and patterns. Their heels, at least double the height of Makala's, don't slow down their walking.

Ash tightens his lips to a closed-mouth smile and nods at guests. Makala grabs onto Ash's shoulder when she reaches him.

'You gave it your best shot. There are flip flops in the car.' He grins and pulls her along through the hedges where Barrow and Daphne wait.

'You think I can walk back to the car? The invitation had a map but no mention of treacherous terrain.' Makala feigns a hand across her forehead and a deep breath. 'Did you really put flip flops in the car?' She furrows her brow.

'Flip flops?' Barrow asks when he's within earshot.

'Does it count if I left them in the boot the last time we went to the beach?' Ash winks.

Daphne chuckles politely, her phone in her hand.

They walk through the gap in hedges and stand to the side as guests slowly dribble into the ceremony. A musician tunes a guitar and a singer hums, holding an off microphone under a white tent. In the centre of the outdoor area is a large white archway surrounded by large vases filled with pale pink flowers. Guests begin to fill the plastic clear chairs facing the archway. Barrow nods towards the chairs in the front row.

'Please, sit. We'll be welcoming the bride soon,' a person wearing a small microphone attached to their flowy yellow top says.

The musicians play an acoustic version of a pop song that was on the radio five years ago. Makala mouths the lyrics to herself, and Ash shakes his head with an amused smile. The groom and his groomsmen stroll over from the building hidden from the other side of the hedges.

The guitar slows down to a soft ballad as bridesmaids in silver satin dresses walk up the aisle. Behind them, Renee beams, her golden-brown hair in ringlets around her face and the rest tied back and covered by a white veil, with Sophie and Jo, dressed in matching white suits, on either side. Makala becomes misty-eyed seeing tears sliding around Sophie and Jo's big smiles. Makala pulls out her tissue packet and Barrow leans over Ash with his hand outstretched for some tissues.

Jo and Sophie sit beside Daphne close to the aisle. Sophie drapes her jacket, a flower pinned to the lapel, over her daughter's shoulders. Daphne is just a year shy of the age her mother fell pregnant with Makala. Her mother never lets her forget how hard it was to be a single teen mum, but she was so grateful to 'beat' teen pregnancy herself that she barely registers how young that age is to be responsible for a living person. She looks at Daphne and can't see her carrying a baby. Nor herself, now twenty-two years old, doing primary school drop-offs alongside parents around a decade older than her. She didn't even cope with helping her mum through her issues.

A speaker whines with the metallic sound of the microphone feedback, startling Makala out of her thoughts. Guests politely laugh as the bride and groom use the moment to blink away tears before returning to reciting their vows. During the exchange of the rings, Barrow pats his eyes.

As everyone stands to congratulate the couple, the photographer guides everyone into family and friend photos. Sophie and Jo hug Renee from either side and kiss her cheeks. Makala finds it so odd to see kisses, even just on the cheek, between family.

'My makeup!' Renee protests. Her new husband pats her cheeks and she relaxes her shoulders with a smile.

The photographer calls for family and Ash joins his parents and siblings for a few photos. Makala distracts herself from the pang of jealousy by admiring how handsome Ash looks in his grey suit, his green tie matching her dress.

'Makala, family picture! Get in!' Jo waves at her. Makala's eyes open wide. She drops her purse on the seats and rushes over to them.

'Took you ten minutes to go that distance before,' Ash whispers to her as he wraps his arm around her waist.

'Yoga!' the photographer calls for them to repeat for the picture. Jo's big laugh hollers, pushing everyone to join in and the photographer grins wide at capturing the moment.

✳

Jo and Renee dance to an ABBA song Jo probably charmed the DJ to play so early in the reception. The light-up square dancefloor in front of the bridal table isn't lit up yet but Jo and Renee bop and sing to 'Mamma Mia' like they're on Broadway. Makala remembers her mum tried a similar thing at her twenty-first birthday. It was the next big thing she saved for all on her own after her overseas trip, but her mum tried to live all the milestone parties she missed growing up in one night, Mikala's night.

Sophie talks to the reception emcee beside the family table where Daphne, Barrow, Ash, and Makala quietly pick at their plates from the charcuterie board. The table is lined with a white tablecloth and a native floral bouquet in a long gold vase encircled by three tall electric candles as the centrepiece. Makala pockets the placeholders with her and Ash's names in her purse.

'Wine?' a server with a curly blonde mullet offers Ash and Makala with a friendly smile.

'Yes. White, please,' Ash says, and Makala shakes her head quickly to decline, her cheeks a little pink.

Ash chuckles at his girlfriend's inability to respond to women with edgy haircuts and tattoos. Makala's bi panic arises at anyone sharing features with her sexual awakening,

Miley Cyrus.

The ABBA song fades out as the emcee approaches the dancefloor.

'Give it up for the bride and her mum, Jo!' They gesture to them as Jo grapevines to her seat and Renee's husband escorts her to the centre of the bridal table and hands her a glass of champagne.

'Now, it may seem funny to all of you, but nothing upsets a bride more than a phone going off during speeches, so please silence your calls, alarms and any sounds your phone may make while taking videos.' The emcee points around the room, a couple of phones beeping as attendees check them. 'Remember, we have a videographer capturing this if you'd like to give your phone a break.'

Makala slips her phone out of her overstuffed purse to check it, and a message appears on the locked screen from her mum:

> *Sweetie, I really want to talk. I'm seeing a therapist and working on myself. I'm not asking for forgiveness but*

The text cuts off in the incoming message window. She wipes the message off the screen and rams the phone back in her purse. Makala thought about blocking her mum's calls when she stopped talking to her a year ago, but she couldn't quite shake the worry of an emergency. But after months and months of no contact, she cares little about one.

Ash and Barrow are placing bets on how many times Jo curses and apologises for it in her speech. Makala stares up at the bouquet. She counts the flowers and names the colours, breathing deeply. *Five large white flowers. Big breath in. Three small white flowers. Big breath out. Four different types of green leaves. Big breath in and out.*

The back of her chair is to the bridal table, so she must turn around to prevent alerting Ash of her worry at his family's special occasion. She turns her chair around and pulls at the thread of her dress, then slaps her own hand away. *It already looks so cheap*, her mother's hypercritical voice creeps into her ear.

The speeches begin but the sounds of people talking and attendees clapping are distant. She focuses on what shade of green her dress is. *Is it teal? Or maybe emerald? Teal or emerald? Emerald or teal green? My future bridesmaid party could wear multiple shades of dark green. My mother would hate that. Would I invite her? Would she show up?*

Makala grips tightly at her knee where her dress ends. She traces her hands along the seam and looks up at Sophie delivering her speech. Makala squints at Sophie's face, her face warmly glowing under the fairy lights, and listens to her caring mother's voice.

'It was always just me and Daphne against the world.' Sophie tucks a loose blonde hair behind her ear. 'But when I met Jo, Renee, you were the biggest cheerleader for our happiness.'

Makala tried not to gloat about her happiness. Her mum would always bring it back to her lost youth.

'When you talked about Craig, I knew you felt the same way I do about your mum and I had to be—' Sophie sniffles and wipes at a tear under her eyes, and Jo beside her rubs Sophie's back. 'Ah! I promised Daphne I wouldn't embarrass her during the speeches.' Sophie points to Daphne who covers her face with an electric candle from the table. Many people around the room laugh but Makala's face is red and her lips tremble.

'I had to be *your* cheerleader, for your love. And I really am. I love you, Renee and Craig,' Sophie continues.

Makala blinks away tears, recalling her mum telling her Ash would leave her, like men do.

'To the happy couple!' Sophie raises her glass out then

sips it, and everyone, including Daphne with her water, follows her. Makala's glass shakes in her hand, and she grabs onto her wrist with her spare hand. She doesn't sip her water.

'I love you, Mum.' Renee hugs Sophie tightly. Jo wraps her arms around both of them. If Makala wasn't at a table so close she wouldn't have heard it.

Renee is living her dream. Makala's stomach cramps. The volume of the attendees in this echoing building covers her whimpering. Her body tenses and she tries to hold that tension for a second and release it, hold it and release it, hold and... But it doesn't release. She launches from her seat, a little shaky, and walks to the exit while everyone claps and some people stand, for Sophie's speech.

Hot tears spill out of Makala's eyes as she leaves the reception. Her heels kick up a few pebbles from the pathway and she catches herself losing her balance. *Why does this wedding destination love paths so hazardous to drunk and emotional people?*

She pulls her heels off, cursing leaving the sand-covered flip flops in the car, and the buckle of her second shoe breaks. She feels a guttural scream rising inside her but she's too close to the wide doors, a dance hit now loudly pumping everyone into the night.

She shivers walking down the path, regretting leaving Ash's jacket on the seat, as her bare feet touch the cold pebbles, and she heads for the nature strip by the driveway. She drops to the grass and opens her mouth to scream but it's a soft wail. She rips the lashes off her eyelids, and the tears pooling at her eyes sting her.

'Makala, Makala,' Ash calls out as he lightly jogs down the pebble path. 'Makala?'

The night conceals the burrowed eyebrows he gets when he's concerned but she can hear his voice hesitate. Ash doesn't hesitate.

'I'm sorry... Go back... Family... Important,' Makala blubbers.

He sits beside her and pulls her into his chest.

'Makeup.' Ash pulls her head up and looks in his eyes with her makeup smeared slightly under her eyes and her foundation sticky from tears.

'I'm sure I've got some food on this shirt. You know I'm not a fan of white anyway.' He pulls her head into his chest.

She heaves her body up and down as they sit in the sound of her sobbing and breathing. As she slows down, he kisses her on top of her head a couple of times.

'Your family makes it look so easy,' Makala whispers into his chest.

'What?' He bows his head on her shoulder.

'Showing up and loving each other.' Makala breathes in a big snot through her nose and sucks her bottom lip as she pushes herself out of his chest and upright. 'My mum wants to try again but I don't want to. I feel like I'm betraying that inner child that just wants her mum there all the time.' This close she can see his large brows knitted together in the darkness.

'Well, you wouldn't expect a kid to forgive her mum.' He relaxes his face. 'When we have our own wedding one day, you'll see how much of *our* family shows up for us.'

Makala's face scrunches up again as a lump rises in her throat.

'You'll get the traditional deal you didn't have. Big family wedding, white picket fence, buddles of joy.' He leans his head to the side and softly smiles. 'Oh no, don't tell me you've changed your mind,' he laughs.

She takes a big breath out to soothe her crying.

'I'm pregnant.'

Of Simpler Times
by Eugene Tabios

I. Ablution

Short, subtle taps. There's a sort of rhythm as they drop. I wonder if that's why I've always loved the rain. The rain is me smelling the blooming moist grass. The rain is me running through the greenery towards the house. The rain is me warming myself on the fireplace as Ma brings over hot chocolate. The rain is… maybe I wasn't really thinking about the rain.

'Black coffee, please.'

The barista nods and turns his back to the counter. The café, in all its gold-like shimmer, caught my eye among the spectres of white and red dancing around me as I ran for shelter. Maybe the huge 'Grand Opening' sign also helped.

I didn't mind getting wet, but my tool of the trade needs care—and this laptop is the one thing that keeps me close to home. Rachel and I did bring a few more things to the city while moving, but for the most part, I am as new and as lost as this shop is within this grey metropolis. I sit down around the corner table, right behind the brick wall adjacent to the door. I take a sip from my coffee.

'Excuse me, can I have some sugar cubes?'

Holding one piece, I let the coffee seep through the cube. *Will I ever be this cube*, I muse, *soluble to the world around it*? I turn my head to stare at the warm droplights over the counter, then back outside. As if a camera on long exposure, I see not cars but mere trails of colour flashing by. Silhouettes of people walk in patterns, on autopilot. I take another sip.

The coffee is sweeter.

I pull out another tissue after wiping away residue from my lips. It'd be fun to write without a screen for a change. The glow of the café's lights reminds me of the fireplace at home.

> *aromatic blend*
> *amid splashes in the rain—*
> *cities spring to life*

Leaving the tissue behind, I feel eager to run against the storm. If a small amount of sugar can make a difference, surely I can make a blend I'm satisfied with.

'Ah—'

II. Two Windmills

'—choo!'

My hand reaches my face just in time. I look around to see if anyone is watching, then sigh with relief. I remember we've got no customers.

> *very humid and*
> *salty air through dark lenses—*
> *bright summer noontime*

Might be the new makeover that's got me sneezing. On the wall, alongside the haiku and a picture of another café (which Miss Aurora says is from Venice), are framed posters of her, Al's, and my favourite movies that now greet the customers when they come in.

'Those are some nice posters you got there,' one lady says as she goes up to the counter. 'You watch any of them?'

'I've only seen *Amélie*.'

I swear I see her glasses light up.

'I love that film!' She holds my hands, but then lets go. 'Sorry, got excited.'

I smile back in response. 'Favourite scene?'

'That part with the phone booth had me crying on end. What about you?' I'm pretty sure her glasses are glowing or something.

'Amélie enjoying the little things in life got to me.'

'Ah, like the crème brûlée?'

I nod.

'Uh-huh,' the lady says, stroking her chin. 'Know what? Get me one of those and an espresso.'

Al simply hands me two cups and points at the customer's table while staring at me. I shrug.

I sit next to the customer, who is looking around the café. 'On vacation?'

She stops halfway through her sip. 'Mm? No, no, I live nearby. I'm just surprised I've never been here ever.' She says she has recently arrived from an excursion and is looking for a stopover before going home. 'I'm a researcher, you see, so I'm always out on trips. Maybe that's why I never noticed...'

We both drink. 'At least you're still discovering something new here,' I joke.

She grins, almost approvingly. 'My name's Rachel,' she says, her hand reaching out to me.

'Dawn.'

A ding comes from the counter. The crème brûlée is ready. I stand up, but not before another sip.

III. Another Autumn Afternoon

'Thanks, Al.' My ears perk up at the sound of my spoon cracking the crust. 'This is never not delightful.'

'Glad to have served you all these years, boss.' Al's been growing out his beard over the months, something he never really did ever while he worked here. Guess he's trying to live up to the grandpa role. 'Now if only Dawn had let me handle the reception…'

'Oh, knock off it. She was being considerate, you know.'

'A wedding is no big deal, boss. I still got it in me.'

'You want to retire sooner?'

Silence. We both stare out the glass windows, with reddish foliage adorning the pavement bordering the towering structures and the pink twilit sky. I take a scoop out of the crème brûlée.

'Al, do we get wiser when we get older, or just wistful?' I turn to him.

He stares up at the decorative lights on the ceiling. The glint on his facial hair really reveals his age. 'Maybe both,' he concludes. 'The wiser we get, the lonelier we become.'

I stay around for a bit after Al leaves. Once again it is me and this place, floating along this ocean of skyscrapers. Shutting my eyes, I can vividly see the younger me in the office, slamming my resignation letter on the boss's desk. I took my leave as the paperwork flew out like confetti.

A final scoop of crème into my lips. I open my eyes.

Suddenly, leaves flutter in the air. Suddenly, I am sitting in stark sunlight, accompanied by the shadows of doves taking flight from the basilica. Suddenly, I am in the Venetian piazza all over again—yet as quick as this realisation, suddenly, I am back in my own world.

As I walk away, I keep turning back, even though I know the café will still be there. A final glimpse lets me read this season's haiku:

> *the end births new days*
> *yet moments linger in time—*
> *leaves fall on the road*

IV. Backwards, Forwards

> *light through frosted glass*
> *striking past the wispy sighs—*
> *fresh winter morning*

...is what I think the rightmost frame says, at least to the extent of my vision from the fogged-up windows. The keys tinkle audibly through the whistling wind as I reach for the doorknob. After a moment of fumbling around the darkness, I find the switch.

For a closed café, it sure looks active. Tables are lined up as if waiting for me to sit at them, and the lights around the counter seem to be expecting Grandpa anytime soon. I did hear that the old owner kept this place clean up until her death, but not to this extent.

My eyes drift towards the brick accent walls that complement the dirty white interior. On the left is the counter shelf where coffee machines and cups used to be, entrenched under the café's serif-designed name—a metal-plated text in lowercase accompanied by an unmoving clock. On the right, the bricks seem to serve as mere borders to the number of frames on the wall, an assortment of images from days past: of albums that Grandpa danced to, of other cafés around the world, of films of perceived reality, of the buildings that lived here, of poems, of customers, of the trio that simply belonged, and still do. Of memories.

Of simpler times, like the name of the place.

I rest on one of the tables after checking around for potential areas that need critical fixing. At the most, I'll be able to run the place again as early as next week. I yawn for a bit. Outside, car lights float like lanterns on a procession, flashing upon Grandpa's *2001: A Space Odyssey* poster. Snow begins to fall, even though the sun is rising. I feel warm, nonetheless.

*to uncover and
(re)discover*

Birthday
by Dante DeBono

Each year my grandma gifts me
a new pot and a plant to put in it.

I wonder what she means.

the song of the poppy
seeds unwashed and floating
turn the water yellow, sallow
stick me up against the tiled floor
wings
       heavy
waterlogged body, mind, heart departed
fear humming like a mechanism of the skin
sloughing off in waves under
the pounding fire
of the shower

here she is:
smiling at a stranger
that remembers her from
three, four, five years
before
she had a name again
or a place to go where it didn't sting
to hear it spoken
aloud with love injected along its length
so that it flowed like water
off a tongue that thirsted
while safety beckoned
from the doorway of a great
lighthouse

I'm scared to go in

I'll have to forge papers
smudge out sharp edges
make myself right-sized
to fill out the needy story

I'm a blur out here
in the rain:
three-year-old
with a make-believe basket
collecting
stars
out of a shallow sky

(song of the poppy)
by Lily Roberts

Desiderium
by Anneliese Abela

Sometimes the juice is green. Celery, spinach, apple, lemon and ginger. Sometimes he throws a few carrots in, and it turns out orange. Or a handful of berries, and it turns out red. Whatever colour, he gulps it down in one go. A grimace brushes his face for the slightest moment before he smiles and smacks his lips as if it's the best thing he's ever tasted.

And then he looks at me, a look that says, 'This is going to work.'

Because it has to. All of it together—the supplements, the juice, the infusions, the diet, the meditation and experimental treatments—it's all got to work.

Before we were born, he'd drive his old panel van to the sea, where the jagged skeleton of an old shipwreck rests on the sand. He dragged his diving gear down rocky cliffs towards the churning ocean. Sea-green waves pulled him in. He dived beneath the surface, strong lungs letting him venture deep.

He laid his catch of orange crayfish beside his oxygen tank, the wind rustling scrub grass and drying the salty curls atop his head. Fresh freckles were already forming on his cheeks. He zipped the back of his diving suit and turned to face the ocean, ready to go again.

I remember the comforting smell of wax polish, and the scuff of a boar bristle brush on his boots, his ironed dress blues and shining gold badges, the pattern of khaki camouflage and a felt slouch hat. I hear the scrape of a shovel to clear snow from our driveway, see the blue glow of Christmas lights strung like icicles from the roof. He pushes us down the frozen hill on plastic sleds, our entire world as sparkling as untouched snow beneath the twilight glimmer of watercolour skies.

He books an appointment with the dentist to fix a throbbing ache in his tooth. The unearthed tumour crowds his sinus, and it takes eleven hours to cut it from his face. She sits beside him through it all, refusing to leave his side despite the ache in her back from the stiff hospital chair. His cheekbone is replaced by silvery titanium, the socket of his eye hollowed and neck left swollen. Rounds of chemotherapy and radiation destroy whatever's left. His hair falls and his face changes, but his brown eyes still shine with a hopeful glint, the corner of his mouth lifting in a mischievous smile. A smile of survival.

Three years into his remission, I hear the sharp intake of breath as he moves ahead of me, hiking boots climbing eternal stone steps. The wall is steep, winding on forever through endless Chinese forests around us. I place my own feet in the weathered grooves of a thousand others and look out over emerald pines bathed in overhanging mist. I clutch at a stitch in my side.

'I can't go any further. This is high enough.'

He shakes his head and holds my hand as we continue towards the highest lookout tower. 'It'll be worth it for the view,' he says, 'to be able to say we did it.'

We reach the tower together. The top of the wall, the top of the world—each inhale of mountain air stabbing our chests. Six tumours grow like stalactites in his lungs.

Eight to twelve months. That's what the doctors say. They've caught it too late. It's in his bones, his spine, his bloodstream. There's nothing to be done. He drives the long way home, her hand a reassuring weight on his thigh. They both wonder how they'll tell us.

The chemo and radiation come first, to try and shrink the mutinous cells that spill through his veins and betray every inch of his body. Then all that's left to do is wait for the day he slips away, to memorise the sight of his face and the feel of his hands and the sound of his voice.

Eight to twelve months. It's not good enough, not long enough. He won't give in without a fight. It's not just his body that needs healing. He knows it's his mind and spirit too. The whole of a human being, not just organs and bones and blood.

He sits in the quiet peace of meditation, thumbs and fingertips pressed together above his knees. Everything slows, the outside world stilling to a murmured hush, and he listens to what his soul tries to tell him. He wakes me at dawn to travel with him to the markets, to gather baskets of fresh produce heaved off farm trucks. The kitchen counter is hidden beneath his state-of-the-art juicer, the entire house filled with its mechanical hum as each fruit and vegetable is blended to pulp. Vibrant greens and reds and oranges—the colours of life returning to his veins. He searches far and wide for new medicines and untried treatments, and meets with others fighting for survival, trying everything offered to him and throwing himself all in.

He writes it all down, filling pages upon pages with his scattered script and sketches, spilling each optimistic, desperate and heartbroken thought in rich blue calligrapher's ink.

And it starts to work. The eighth-month mark passes, and then the twelfth—his body still crowded with tumours but his health and spirit soaring. He doesn't look like he's going anywhere in a hurry.

Twenty months on, and I can still clasp his hand, still see the tears in his eyes when he laughs too hard. An entire epoch of life squeezed into the extra time he has stolen.

I wonder now whether I was selfish, to think it still was not enough.

We climb down the rickety staircase built into the cliff face, the wooden boards creaking and slippery with rot. High tide floods the beach, the ocean pouring her own heartache over the shipwreck beside us. Iron beams lay exposed like the fossilised ribcage of a whale, left for a century to dissolve and melt into the sand.

We scoop handfuls of his ashes and scatter them on the wind, throw them over the rusted hull of the ship and tangled piles of seaweed washed in with the tide. Beneath the snarl of seaside winds, the guitar solo of Pink Floyd's *Wish You Were Here* echoes from our pockets. A thunderous wave breaks and crashes the surf and carries him back once more into the familiar depths of the ocean.

And as my memories fade and he drifts further away, I'm still unsure how to recover from the loss of him. I cling to grief like the plastic handles of a sled as I soar down a snow-capped hill, his laughter ringing in the air behind me. The cold burns my fingertips, but I won't let go.

Because I just want him back, making green juice in the kitchen, smiling at me with that hopeful glint of survival in his eyes.

Spark an Interest
by Dante DeBono

She spends Sundays at her grandparents' house, clumsy feet carrying her up and down expansive hallways and through the flowering garden. A whirlwind on arrival, it's not long before she's counting all the pretty leadlight windows and then all the plain ones, before rushing outside to pick a scraggly bouquet of daisies and lavender. The stems are a jagged line of uneven lengths, bruised slightly by her indelicate grip. They bring a smile to her grandma's face regardless, earning the esteemed position of centrepiece on the dining room table. When she's called inside for lunch and comes running to eat peanut butter and jam sandwiches with her nan, she stares at the glass vase of flowers with a proud grin tugging at the corners of her sticky, crumb-covered mouth.

'Take a plate to your grandfather, would you, darling?'

Happily, she picks it up, balancing the blue dish in between her hands as she walks to his study at a much more measured pace. When she gets to the door it's waiting, left ajar so she can bump it wider with one grass-stained foot before announcing herself.

'Sandwiches!' she calls out, already headed towards the desk her Pa is sitting at, back hunched over his papers as he scribbles out notes. His illegible writing looks like black squiggles to her, but she pretends to read them over with a quick glance anyway, humming as if she understands.

'Thank you, my dear,' he says, taking the plate from her and brushing a quick kiss on the top of her head.

He doesn't dismiss her, so she stays in the room, roaming around and staring guilelessly. There are framed pictures hanging on the walls—time having stolen the colours from the faded photos—and a single window that overlooks the garden she was zooming through earlier. But mostly there are books. Stacks and stacks and shelves, all full of them. The room emanates the musty smell of pressed pages and ink, the same scent that always follows her grandfather, encloses her in his warm hugs, and lingers on his coat. With one, single finger, she travels the length of the room, feeling the uneven spines that line the bottom-most shelf that she's able to reach. She stops at a thick volume, leather-bound and shining, the gold letters reflecting in her eye. It takes a pretty big tug, but she manages to dislodge the book from its place on the shelf, and it tumbles out onto the carpeted floor, landing on its back with a dull thud. She drops down to sit and starts sounding out the embossed title.

'Lll. Lee. Le-a. Lee-av.'

'Leaves,' comes the amused voice of her grandpa, watching her with a smile as he eats his lunch.

'Leaves,' she dutifully repeats, turning back to the book. 'Of.'

Her gaze flicks up quickly for a reassuring nod before she continues.

'Leaves of... grrah. Grass. Leaves of Grass.'

'Very good,' Pa compliments.

'Is it just about grass?' she asks.

'Yes and no.'

He laughs at her scrunched-up nose, confused and displeased by his inadequate response. *How could I answer the child?*

'It's a book of old poems,' he offers.

'Like Dr Suess?'

'A bit, yes. Though there are many more words and far fewer pictures.'

'Why would they do that?'

'Well, the words are the important bit. They're the part

that makes the stories.'

'The bit you read.'

'Yes, the bit you read. But you also think about the words while you're doing it, feel things because of them. Your imagination plays with them, can take them further than what's on the page. And they can mean something different to whoever is reading them, even though they always say the same thing.'

'How do they do that?' she asks him.

He leans in, conspiratorially. 'It's the magic of words.'

Her expression takes on the kind of wonderment reserved for the young. With a throaty chuckle, he rises with his now-empty plate and leaves her to ponder over the book, her childish fingers tracing the deep green cover reverently.

When her parents come to collect her in the evening, he will send it home in her hands.

I was a dancer
who always forgot to imagine my own
skeleton arranged in space: those holy bones
kept aloft like wind chimes
by living tissue and the grit of angels

to have kept it that simple
when I was a cloud
of mere want, held apart by grey boxes,
hardwood floors, and shouting men
would have been impossible

the body was a thing only:
no nourishment
outside the scheduled hours, only casting death
or dark looks
at mirrors that told skewed truths

outside, the sharp blades of grass
cut my cheek
into four thousand tears

I never saw a holly hock
or craved the simple touch of another girl
shorter than me, until later, when
her rough fruit skin peeled under my wet thumb
to reveal sacred flesh
shining pomegranate seeds

(unbidden)
by Lily Roberts

Fresh Inspiration
by Aden Burg

The boy stopped. He was stuck. His formation was at an impasse. The opponent was one move from breaking through with a joint attack from his bishop and silver general. The boy took a deep breath. He closed his eyes and emptied his thoughts. Once clarity had returned to him, his eyes fixated on the board. Upon lengthy examination, the boy found that even if he managed to avoid checkmate, he would lose the advantage and then be placed in a precarious position. His opponent would have at least two promoted pieces ready to attack. The boy moved his hand over his bishop.

I could counter his silver general with this bishop, which would then be defended by my rook...

The boy wavered, his hand almost brushed against his bishop, held in the wooden tringle that laid quietly upon the board. However, his hand pulled back as his eyes moved to the man's backline. There, laid a single lancer that was elegantly vertically aligned with the man's silver general.

No, he would counter with his lancer... It's lying in wait for this very moment.

The boy pulled back his hand. His eyes skirted across the board.

'Good observation,' the man remarked. The boy merely nodded. He was grateful for the compliment, yet his focus on the board was undiluted. His eyes darted across all the squares that formed the board. The man silently sat, his eyes level and unmoving. The boy moved his hand to his rook.

No, he'll checkmate in two moves.

To his knight.

I will be put in check, forced to sacrifice my gold general and bishop to survive checkmate.

His gold general.

That will merely prolong the game five moves, then he will squarely checkmate me.

Again and again, the boy looked, but he found no way to advance.

I guess that's to be expected though... He has been playing this game his whole life... After all, I've never beaten him. Not ever. How many games has it been? Fifty? Sixty? Seventy or Eighty? Maybe even a hundred... Even so... I can't just...

The boy took a sip of green tea. His eyes did not move from the board. However, as he took this simple sip of tea, the world came into sharp clarity. The smooth texture of the wooden teacup, the soft bitterness of the tea that moved down his throat, the hum of the jazz in the background, the white table the board was upon, and his opponent who waited ever so patiently for the boy. With this clarity, the boy realised that this whole game, he had only played in response to the man. The man had taught him everything about Shogi: the rules, the movement, the strategies, the formation, and the counters. So, every time they had played, the boy had always played in response to the man. When the man played defensively, the boy used an offensive strategy. Conversely, such as with this game, when the man played offensively, the boy played defensively. Because of this, the opponent could always predict the boy's moves. The man could always see the limitations, counters, and openings of the boy's strategies and formations. The boy realised after all that he was merely matching his opponent's moves with the corresponding opposite dynamic. As a result, the man would take his time, he would carefully wait and observe the boy. The boy always knew that his defeat was close at hand in these moments, that was why he had convinced himself of his limited options. The man's eyes followed the fretting boy. He watched as the boy frenetically worked to avoid checkmate. Then, the man would strike, methodically slicing his way to a careful victory.

Of course, he noticed the opening of my formation, that it doesn't defend outside of the formation itself and that it leaves a silver general vulnerable. By taking that, he gets a piece close enough to disturb the formation and then is able to drop that general right in the middle of it... Yeah, all I was doing was responding to him. So, I'll stop that right now and cease this defence. Right now, I'll show him my own Shogi, the unyielding Tiger!

The boy could not help but smile. He could not help but be filled with immense joy and gratitude. In this moment of elation, he moved the gold general that had remained in the back of defensive formation one space forward. His defensive Turtle formation had been shattered and reformed as a counteroffensive Tiger formation. His opponent was silent for a moment, he blinked just once and then he smiled.

'Interesting,' the opponent replied before taking the boy's first silver general and promoting his own silver general. The boy countered with his knight. Take, take, take and promotion, take and check, take, take, drop, take, take, take, move and check, take, move, move, take, drop, move, drop, take, move and promotion, move, take, move and promotion.

Until this point, the game had been slow and focused, a calm exchange that had taken nearly half an hour to reach the point they were currently inhabiting. Prior to this, each move had been slow and thoughtful. Each clack of the board represented a precious and careful thought that each player held within himself. The slow momentum of which was shattered, as the last twenty-nine moves had all occurred in the blink of an eye. Each move had been swiftly signalled by the clicking of each piece against the board. It was a brief symphony of movement. It was a masterpiece that only these two would ever know. At the end of this movement, the man found himself on the brink of checkmate. The boy had not only managed to push the man back and counterattack, but to push up a promoted rook, a promoted lance, and a gold general to make the final attack. The man only had his rook, one lance, six pawns, and two silver generals to defend against checkmate with. Despite that, the man smiled as he sipped his tea.

Am I pushing him to the edge? Yeah, I'm winning. But, still... He's having fun. Good.

The man had been his Shogi friend for a few months, but the boy had not bested the man even once during that time. Every time without fail, the man had claimed a clear and overwhelming victory. Yet, each time, the boy had improved and gained more skill. The boy had gained new moves, new tactics, new wisdom with each defeat. In this game, the boy's growth had extended even beyond that. His strategic mind had improved vastly from whence it once sat.

'Excellent, your skill and growth are truly wonderful. It has been ten years since anyone has pushed me this far. Thank you very much. Allow me to show you due respect.' The man smiled as he lowered his teacup to the table, rolled his shoulder, and cricked his neck. His body now seemingly looser. His hand reached towards the board, grasped a silver general, and put it one square forward.

That's Climbing Silver! Climbing Silver is a high-risk end game move, one I've never managed to do correctly! But right now, he's doing that move! Every other move of his is so calcu-lated, so precise, and careful. Yet here... I've pushed him that far... Yeah, I've put him far enough he's desperate enough to... No!

The boy gazed at the man. The man smiled back as he retained his cool exterior.

This isn't some bluff. He isn't trying to mess with me or put forward some final desperate attack. No, he's just never had to rely on any moves like this until this point. Right now, I think he's just been inspired to not limit himself anymore because I've grown. He's throwing out everything, but he's still in control and sees a way to defeat me.

The boy smiled back at the man.

I see, so I can't just see this as a last-ditch effort, huh? Ok, so, I can't try to use any normal counters for this either. I'm sure he's already prepared for that. I probably can't try to just use it against him either, since he's probably already seen through that too...

The boy gazed down at the board once more. Upon it, he saw the man's formation anew. It was indeed not a final stand that he saw. Instead, it was a complete reincarnation of a formation, reborn as a Silver Phoenix stratagem. The boy recognised it as a power that was hard to manage, one that could easily be fizzled away. Yet, through his cool gaze, the man had tempered its flames and turned it into a powerful advance. Even so, the boy did not cease smiling, nor did he relent. Rather, he merely moved his promoted lance to check the man's king.

All I can do is show him my Shogi, without relenting to his. All I can do is push forward without a clear notion for him to see through and force him to respond to me. Even then... Can I win? He's clearly grown too. He's able to put forward such a risky move with such control. So, maybe not... But still... I won't know until I show him the full extent of my new Shogi!

Both players were smiling, they had both evolved and changed. They were elated that they were not only playing as a bettered form of themselves, but also against an opponent who was also at their best. To which, they found immense gratitude for one another and the humble green fertiliser which led to such fresh inspiration.

Applying Conté to a Scene
by Lyndal Hordacre Kobayashi

Dense greens and brown fronds ripple up each side of the cartridge paper, reflecting a glittery metallic green aura. Blue conté dust falls from the sky, settling evenly between the top of the page and the bottom, blue glistening particles in the sand, light enough to move with the gentlest of breezes.

More shimmering moments transpire between the image and the swirling blue as the colour begins to move upwards again, towards the top right of the page, spilling outwards in an exploding phosphorescence.

Rocks cluster lower on the page. They float downwards, gaining weight as they sink to the base of a path, which leads away into the distance. The rocks are an unusual ochre colour. Some are tinged with a light pink, mauve shade which gives distinction to their irregular semi geometrical surfaces.

Pastel blue now surrounds them, having fallen in clumps against their heavy shapes.

The central rock is even and smooth. I flatten my hand against it. There is a slight indentation in the middle. My hand washes into the pool of water which rests there, disrupting the reflection of the metallic green sky and the glistening particles.

There is silence, apart from the waves building up and thrashing in parallel lines along the shore, silvery-white foam catching sparkling rainbow colours as it stretches upwards and outwards, threading around the horseshoe shape of the bay.

A jolt, the air is disrupted and swept upwards by a figure dismantling the scene as he whizzes past.

Green Bay
by Evan Jarrett

Dean kissed Stacy on the head. She didn't stir. He climbed out of bed and chucked on his boardies. The first ray of the day cut through the palms lining the driveway as he loaded his board onto Amy, their lime-green 1972 Kombi. She started on the third go. The driveway was steep and muddy, puddles from last night's storm filling the ruts. Amy chugged up it without complaint. Dean smiled as he turned onto the road, heading downhill. A green-tinted mist floated above the treetops in the valley.

'Wow, man!'

It was almost an hour's drive to this spot, or so he'd been told, and it was easy to miss. Dean scanned the verge. The road got narrower and sandier. Palm fronds caressed Amy from both sides. Then he saw it, a rock cairn about a metre tall. It was decorated with green spirals. He turned left.

Untold time passed as Amy chugged down the track. The sun was strong now, biting, and the forest was soaking up every bit of it. Fleshy emerald leaves spread themselves out, reaching up, embracing it. The track ended in a clearing. It looked like it had been months since anyone had been here—not a tyre track to be seen—and the grass was up to the mudguards. A large kangaroo made an appearance, looking at them with curiosity rather than fear, before bounding inland along an animal trail. A hawk circled above. Dean turned off Amy. She ran on a few turns then went silent. Outside, the cicadas hissed.

Dean rummaged through the glove box. He pulled out a rusty tin. It was filled with scraggly, leafy weed that smelled like mango. He rolled a spliff. He sat for a while, looking around, before hopping out of Amy. He could hear the surf in the distance, just, but the bush was louder. It was difficult to see, but there was a small opening in the shrubs ahead and what looked like a sand track. It was wider than the animal tracks heading inland, and a rock cairn sat to one side of it. It too had painted green spirals. Dean grabbed his board off the roof and made tracks.

It was a long way to carry a surfboard, but the thudding crash of the waves grew louder. Dean started smiling, sweat dripping from his brow, he knew what was coming—he could feel it.

'Fuck yeah!' he said, looking ahead.

It was hot and moist. The smell of vegetation and compost mixed with sea spray. After what felt like ages, the track started to climb. Just a single dune lay before him and the beach. At the top, the foliage gave way to sky which soon touched sea—a blue green expanse, heaving. Dean was knackered, but excited.

'Dude!' he said aloud as he surveyed what laid before him.

The bay was horseshoe-shaped, but wider, and lined with rocks at both ends. Tall cliffs marked its outer boundaries. The sand was loose and white, descending steeply into the abyss. Fleshy thick shrubs bordered the beach. A wave crashed. It must have been eight metres, maybe more. Dean made his way down the dune.

There was a large flat rock where the path met the beach. At its centre, was yet another green spiral, this one over a metre across. Dean put down his board and stepped on the rock. He sat in the centre of the spiral. From here, it was possible to gauge the timing of the sets and the true scale of the waves. They seemed to grow and rise as they came in, forming perfect tunnels on approach. Despite the surf, there was barely a breath of wind. He lit his spliff.

He watched the waves and breathed. The sets came in like clockwork. Three metres, five metres, eight metres, then three again. Every wave tunnelled from northeast to southwest.

This spot is even better than he said, he thought to himself. He grabbed his board and ran in.

✳

Stacy dropped the needle on Billy Thorpe and the Aztecs and lit some incense. Dean would be up soon, and some old friends were coming over. They said they were bringing someone else too. She gave the place a bit of a clean—a damp cloth and a cheap straw broom. Then she danced. She loved to dance.

'Hey babe,' Dean said over the music, his figure silhouetted by the morning sun.

'You're up late,' she said.

'Few too many Bundys last night,' he said, smirking.

She danced towards him. Dean kissed her.

'What's all this,' he said, looking around at a much tidier house.

'Robbo and Cassie are coming over, remember? And some friend of theirs. Guru or Garry? I swear they said Guru.'

'Dude!' he said. 'Did they say what time?'

'You don't even remember, do you?' she said, smiling.

He smirked.

'I don't know. They said this arvo some time, but who knows. I just wanted the place to look nice,' Amy said.

'Fair call,' Dean said. 'Would you like a smoothie?'

'Thanks, babe.'

Dean headed outside. The sun was bright. He walked over to the veggie patch, bidding good morning to the hens on his way.

'Bok Bok,' he greeted.

The spinach and kale were glowing in the sun. He had to stop and take it all in.

65

'Wow, man!'

He broke off a few branches. On the way back to the house he grabbed a lime off the tree. It too was glowing. He headed back for the kitchen. He chopped his leafy haul and chucked it in the blender. He added two avocados and some semi-ripe bananas. He finished by squeezing in some lime. He switched on the blender.

'Is Robbo gonna bring his guitar?' Dean said over the blender.

'WHAT?' Amy said.

'IS ROBBO GONNA BRING HIS GUITAR?' Dean said, as the blender cut out.

'Does he go anywhere without it?' Amy said.

Dean pondered over that one.

Dean liked to think he could play bass. He had an old upright he found at a garage sale, and he taught himself how to play it. His rhythm was great, and he loved to jam. He was always just flat of the note though. It didn't bother him much.

Dean poured the thick green liquid into some glasses.

'Smoothie, babe,' he said.

They sat on the wicker lounge and drank it.

✳

The water was cool. It cleared his head. He jumped on his board and paddled. The sets were so consistent, so easy to read. He had no trouble getting out behind the break. Sitting on his board, looking back to shore, he lost himself for a bit.

'Wow, man!'

What laid before his eyes was unbelievable. From this point the bay was framed perfectly, the cliffs at each end almost symmetrical, the sea spray shrouding the foliage. Dean sat for a while, his legs dangling in the water, the sun lighting it—penetrating it—the most soul-hugging aqua green he'd ever seen. He noticed, as the waves lifted him and lowered him—three metres, five metres, eight metres—that the bushland on shore seemed to move in time with the breaks, the palm fronds bending inland, the shrubs following suit. Something came over him.

'COOEE!' he yelled.

It echoed inside of him. He laughed. He felt so incredibly high suddenly, not stoned but *high*. He turned and looked out to sea. An eight-metre wave was coming. The hairs stood up on his neck. Blood flooded his core, and he went belly down and paddled. He paddled like fuck.

He was on it. He was *really* on it. It had him and it was moving him and there was no stopping it. He was a part of it. He was on his feet. The wave started tunnelling from the northeast and he was riding it southwest to west shoreward. He did not miss a beat. Like a batsman on a purple patch or a bass player locked in with a drummer, there was no missing this. He was not going to fall off—no way—impossible. Dean screamed. He screamed gibberish. There was no one who could hear him, and he wouldn't have given two shits if there was. Dean lived for this. The wave tunnelled over him. He soared through. The sea spray filled his lungs and his soul—delicious nurturing salt. The sun had moved a long way to the west. Dean had been out a lot longer than he realised. A lot longer than seemed possible. He didn't care though, not at all.

*

The afternoon had come and gone, and the sun was getting low. Dean was sitting on the porch watching a bird. Its plumage was brilliant—a mix of reds, greens, and blues highlighted by deep blacks. It was tiny and fast. It moved frantically—jerky—and yet somehow relaxed and graceful, as if its size and metabolism had sped up its consciousness, moving to a time frame very dif-

ferent than our own. Dean called it Gonzo. He heard a rattly old wagon struggling up the hill, its engine screaming in low gear. Gonzo flew off.

'That's them, I reckon,' he called out to Stacy who was engrossed in a Mandela she had been painting—a complex floral spiral filled with chaotic symmetry.

She looked up and listened.

'Finally!' she said. 'I'll put on some music.'

The wagon pulled up out the front. The engine turned off. Everything went silent. Then the music started—seventies music—on scratchy vinyl.

'Robbo!' Dean said, as he wandered over to him. 'It's been too long.'

'Sure has, man,' Robbo said.

They gave each other a rough hug.

'Hey, Dean,' Cassie said as she wrangled a woven tote bag out from the footwell.

'I see you guys have been out,' Dean said.

'Yeah, man. We weren't going to, but on the road out to pick up Guru we got side-tracked. The waves looked gnarly.'

'Fuckin' aye,' Dean said, looking at the dreadlocked man with leathery skin who had gotten out of the back seat. Dean was feeling it...

'Oh, yeah. This is Guru,' Robbo said, gesturing towards the man.

'Hello,' Guru said quite slowly, looking past them all. He looked at least sixty. He looked like he had seen and tried it all.

Stacy made her way down. She was already holding a drink.

'Come on in, guys. We've got beers and rum and plenty of munchies.'

'Fuck yeah!' Dean said, smiling at the others. They headed in.

The night was one of those nights that made memories. It was both long and short, eventful and mundane. Drinks flowed, weed was smoked, and there may have been some mushrooms *involved. Nothing of note happened and yet it was life-changing. There was music on. There was a jam—Robbo strummed, and Dean plucked. Guru grabbed a drum and they all melded. Stacy and Cassie danced and laughed. Many festivities occurred, but the most important thing was a conversation. It was one of those early hour conversations where stoned minds and offset sleep turn the everyday into the fantastic. Where an off-hand remark turns into an hour of discussion that starts out philosophical and ends up spiritual. This conversation took place around a fire.*

'Have you ever thought about how surfing is like... about more than just waves, man?' Dean said.

'Well, yeah. I mean, it's about the journey you know. Like the act of actually getting there and what happens along the way. I mean, the people I have met and the stories I could tell, all to catch some waves,' Robbo said.

Dean nodded.

'My dad was a surfie back in the seventies,' Stacy said. 'He told me about the time he went to Tahiti and how it was seen over there. It was a man's game back then, amongst the locals, he reckoned. It was like a sign of male potency, taking on the sea spirits, showing you're man enough to stand up to it all. It was spiritual to them.'

'Sounds kind of sexist,' said Cassie.

They had a bit of a laugh.

The conversation went on for some time. Guru never said a word. He just stared at the fire. Then, after things went quiet for a bit, he spoke.

'I've seen things you know,' he said.

They all seemed stunned by this sudden statement. Guru's face told a story in the firelight. His skin was thickened. His face was gaunt. It was like his skin had been stretched over his bones—only muscle and sinew existing beneath. He was tattooed. There were quite a few. There was a green spiral in the centre of his chest. It spiralled out from his sternum.

'I've surfed all over the world,' he said. 'I've been to Tahiti and Hawaii. Bali and India. I've been all over Oz. At first you think, "Everywhere's the same. It's just the scenery is different." It's only the waves and breaks that differ, and the language spoken on shore, but then you realise that it's not like that at all. Some places connect. Others do not'.

'What do you mean?' Dean said after a period of silence.

'A lot of things. Like, some places connect you to their culture through surfing—like Tahiti or Hawaii, or... even Bondi—others, to the land. There are many like that. But there is one place that connects you in a different way, like no others I've ever been to. It connects you to everything, man, like everything.'

He placed his fingers in the centre of his spiral as he said this.

'What do you mean when you say everything?' Dean said.

'There are no words that can describe it. You have to get on a wave and experience it,' Guru said.

By chance or not, Jimmy Hendrix came on in the house, asking everyone if they were... Experienced.

Dean prodded him further. He was fascinated. He had to know. What he found out was that this place was not far. It was only about an hour. It was a secret. He needed to look for the rock cairns and the spiral. Guru kept pointing to his spiral. Everyone crashed out. Dean didn't. He sat up and watched the fire burn out. He fell asleep outside to the sound of morning birds.

✻

Hours passed—or not. It didn't matter. The sets kept coming. Dean never missed one. The sun was over the land now, backlighting the bushland, but high enough that he had to squint to see it. The surf lulled. Dean turned his board and looked out at sea, trying to get a feel for things. This was usually a sign that it was time to head in, but not this time.

He saw it coming just as those thoughts entered his mind. It was massive—scary big.

'Wow, man!' he said.

Before he had time to think any further it was on him. He was paddling—paddling like fuck! It picked him up and pushed him along, tunnelling over him like a mountain. The wind rushed past him, water, salt, ozone—penetrating him. He wasn't missing this one either. Then he saw it. He also *felt* it. A green glow in the sky, rising from beyond the bushland. It kept rising and growing, like mist but somehow fluorescing. It formed a beautiful spiral. His chest started burning.

'Dude!'

He fell off. Water crashed around him and over him. He was underwater and tumbling. He crashed into the sand. The world disappeared, except for the spiral. That stayed. That would never leave.

He was laying on his back. What remained of the sun warmed his skin as he stirred in the sand. His head pounded. He willed himself up. The waves had pretty much disappeared. The water was calm and unthreatening. The water in the bay was glistening and shimmering under the late afternoon sun. Some Pacific Gulls flew overhead, heading out to sea, heading out to find fish. He had no clue where his board was. With some effort, he stood up. He went for a bit of a walk, looking for his board, but never found it. He found himself back at the flat rock and looked on at the spiral painted on it. His memories flooded back.

Dude, what is going on? he thought to himself, as he looked at the bushland, expecting to see it again—or feel it. Nothing. A bird landed on the rock, right in the middle of the spiral. It looked like Gonzo. It may well have *been* Gonzo. It wiggled its tail feathers and flew off. Dean put his hand on his chest. He gazed across the bay, taking it all in, a strange feeling running through him—fear, excitement, love, he couldn't place it. He spotted the entrance to the path, the one across the dune, and felt a sudden urgency to get out of there. Dean made tracks!

*

The following weeks were strange. Dean was troubled by anxious thoughts and bad dreams. Stacy was worried about him.

'You should go to the doctor,' she said regularly.

Dean would tell her the doctor wouldn't understand.

She would remind him that he had hit his head.

He would tell her that it wasn't that.

She would point out that he hadn't been surfing since.

He would tell her to mind her own business. He would word it quite differently though. He would shout it.

The dreams were random and weird, but they all felt the same. They all left him feeling the same way when he got up. Like there was something that he was supposed to do. He had no idea what that was though. For Dean, it was maddening. He started drinking a lot. He would go for long drives and smoke joints, looking out at the sea. He would go into town with the intention of buying a new surfboard, but he never would. He would decide to call Robbo, and see if he could get in touch with Guru, but then he'd find something else to do. He'd wait on the porch for Gonzo. Gonzo would never show. Then one day, Guru rocked up. He just... appeared at the door. He was holding a board.

*

'You found it didn't you?' Guru said. It was the first thing he said.

'I guess I did,' Dean said.

'It got you good, didn't it?' Guru said.

'What is it, man?' Dean said.

'I wish I knew,' Guru said.

'I keep having these dreams. They're freaking me out man! And I don't know what to do. And I keep *feeling* it, like, it's hard to explain but—'

Guru placed his hand in the centre of Dean's chest.

'You're feeling it here, right?'

Dean nodded.

'It nearly killed me,' Dean said. 'This wave, it was fucking gnarly. Like, it wasn't just how big it was. I mean, it was fast—powerful—and then I saw it.'

'The spiral?'

'Yeah, and then I came off. It dumped me, and I guess I got knocked out. I came to onshore and, I dunno, man. It's weird.'

'Have you been back?'

'Nah, man. I lost my board, and... I don't know. I'm scared, man,' Dean said.

'You need to go back. You can take my board. Trust me on this. It needs to tell you something, then you will understand. You hear me?'

'Can you come?'

'No can-do, man. This is something you need to do by yourself,' Guru said.

'Dude...' Dean said.

Guru passed his board to Dean. It was old—off white with sun-fade and salt. It was painted with a single green spiral at its centre. Dean laid it down on the porch. He ran his hands over it.

'Are you sure?' he said, looking into the spiral.

When he looked up Guru was gone.

*

He woke well before dawn. It was a still night—silent and hot—apart from the occasional chatter of fruit bats in the trees. Dean hadn't slept a wink. He got out of bed and put on his boardies. He looked at Stacy. She looked beautiful. He didn't smile though, and he didn't kiss her. He made tracks.

The drive down to Green Bay seemed to take longer than he remembered. There was a silver mist hugging the road that glowed softly in the moonlight. The trees looked sinister, their branches hanging in the breathless air, looking grey and silver, looking like they might conceal something hostile. A figure appeared in the mist. Amy screeched to a halt. A large kangaroo stood in the centre of the road. It hopped to the east, straight past a rock cairn about a metre tall. Dean's chest felt hot.

'I nearly missed it,' he found himself saying aloud. Dean and Amy turned left. The spiral glowed.

Amy chattered along, rocking and rolling over the rocks and ruts, palm fronds and branches screeched along her paint. Her old headlights revealed green amongst the silver, the track narrowing, roughening, getting steeper. They reached the clearing before the dune. Dean turned off Amy and just sat there. He sat there for some time, listening to the slight breeze in the leaves. The birds were stirring, and the moon was setting. Dean pulled out his tin. He tried to roll a spliff, but his hands failed him. He was shaking. His belly was tightening. He put the tin away. The thought crossed his mind to bail. He even put the key back in the barrel. But in the end, he knew what had to be done. He had to get out in the water. He set out to do just that.

Crossing the dune, the bay appeared again before him. It looked a lot less inviting in this light. The moon had almost disappeared behind him, but there was a glow starting to appear on the horizon over the water. In these conditions, the rocks at the ends of the cliffs looked like giant wolf snouts, snapping their jaws at the waves. Dean walked with purpose down the remainder of the track. He walked like a man heading off to battle. He found himself next to the flat rock. The spiral was dull in this light, but still visible. There was a shadow at its centre. He looked closer. It was a bird. A tiny bird. A bird with red, green, and blue plumage, high-lighted by deep blacks. It was dead. It looked like Gonzo. It was Gonzo! Of that, he had no doubt. He felt sick to the pit of his stomach. Then, a thunderous crash caught his attention. He looked out at the waves. They were big. They were scary big! Five metres, eight metres, thirteen metres... Dean looked on, paralysed. In the predawn light, the sea looked like a hungry beast waiting to devour him. He remembered coming to right here last time. He remembered the spiral at the end of the tunnel. He took a deep breath, pushed it out of his mind, and ran out.

After the first wave smashed into the sand, Dean jumped on his board and paddled. He had to be quick if he was going to get behind the break. These waves would smash him otherwise. Luckily, the rhythm was slow. He was out before the next big one came in. The sun was beginning to rise from the ocean. Its dawn rays lit the bay with its soft glow. Dean just sat there, floating, his feet dangling, looking on—waiting. In this light a calm came over him. It was as if the view that lay before him had steeled him to his fate. *Whatever happens from here*, he figured, *will happen. I mean, what a place for it to be so.* Most of all, he was waiting for a sign. He hoped Gonzo wasn't a sign. He sure as fuck didn't want to entertain whatever that meant. He wondered about the spiral. He was terrified of it, hoping to never see it again, and yet, waiting for it, hoping to see it appear. What he did next was all that he could do, all things considered. He turned and looked out to sea and locked onto it, a rising mass, swallowing the infantile sun, rushing, advancing, *coming in...* Dean turned to shore and paddled. He paddled like fuck, man!

He was on it. It had him. Oh, boy, did it have him! He was rising, rushing, progressing forward at great speed, and then he was standing. He was standing at the top of the world. The wave crested over his head, curving, tunnelling, and then he was *in* it, moving across it, salty mist filling him, awakening him. Time stopped. It started as a glow, then it grew into a shimmer. It started to coalesce. This did not occur beyond the shoreline this time, oh no, it was closer than that. There was no such separation and distance for Dean this time. It occurred in front of him, at the end of the tunnel. It spiralled into a brilliant green. He went into it.

There was no sound. There was no wind. There was no movement. Absolute peace is what occurred. He was still there, out on the water, but the wave was gone. He was standing on his board, floating in the stillness. Out at sea was a ship. It was an old wooden sailing ship, its off-white sail hanging limp in the still air. A scurry of activity occurred on board, some men loading muskets, some lowering a rowing boat into the water. On the shore were children—cowering and weeping. The bushland behind was thick with birds. A bulldozer appeared at the end of the bay. It tracked along the beach looking for prey. The bushland was suddenly burning. The ship was gone, but a storm was brewing. Black clouds swirled around, advancing landward. The fire was gone, but the palm trees were bending horizontally. One by one they snapped and fell. A huge smokestack appeared in the sky beyond the now barren dune. It spewed black soot into the atmosphere. There was a flash. A mushroom cloud appeared on the horizon. The dawn light turned pitch black. Suddenly, it wasn't dawn anymore. The sun was high in the sky and it was angry! It was beating down with a ferocity that Dean had to shield himself from. Then it faded back to dawn and a figure appeared on the shore. It was Stacy. She was smiling and pregnant. Then she wasn't. Several children played in the sand. Stacy was now elderly. The children stood up as adults and grabbed shovels. They dug two graves. A flock of Gonzo birds surrounded Dean on his board. They circled frantically, even by their standards, then they flew over the spiral rock and landed upon it. A spiral engulfed the sky, and someone spoke.

'GUIDE THEM,' it said, from both inside and outside of him. There was a green flash, and then he fell both sideways and backward. He fell into absolute nothingness.

Dean opened his eyes. He was laying on the sand. He got up, brushed himself off, and looked out at to sea. It shimmered with peace. He walked around for a while. There was no sign of Guru's board. Gonzo's body was gone. None of this mattered to him at that moment. He knew what he had to do. He had a message he needed to pass on—a message that would long outlive him. He also had a life to live. In a way, that *was* the message. Life. He never returned to Green Bay, but others would—they had to.

A Kinaesthetic Interlude

by Heather Briony McGinn

Green Girl

Oddball girl, summer-skinned and barefoot
Soles like leather
On a quest around the full perimeter of the backyard
To the laundry door
The women's space
The cat's space
The space that's all cool tiles and efficiency
Smells like safety
Quiet
Soft slinky silky tabby cat against strong legs
The hair bleached by January
Boy's legs on a little girl
Already wrong
Too muscular
Too long
Too fast
Too good at high jump, long jump, hurdles, and hockey
Eyes like saucers
Eyes that match the cat's
Hands that match nobody's
Feet that match her brother's, but only up to the ankles
Vampire teeth
Teeth made for plums
Tiny ears so sharply keen they never miss a beat
And an ocean heart wasting away
So far away from the sea
Shackled to the inland
Eucalypts singing
The last blood-free spring

on yearning

self-shrinking madness makes pain possible and rage is the covenant come thru to pilgrimage paid the price with my own feet shredded beyond rejoicing reinvented to the point of hysteria this womb is tired tired tired of tomfoolery and listless afternoons she wants bright burning joy and a scoop of crimson lip-flesh to take away as souvenir of this longing self-shrinking madness

boys in bands

shrouded by mosh pit limbs and a midnight blue velvet
jacket pre-rolled darts in a silver case in the right hand pocket
lighter and lipstick in the left i scribble notes for street press
for unpaid unofficial underground apprenticeship pick up
the bassist and back to his where he performs his noncon-
formity by declaring love for skinny puppy and rude boy
boots he has a foot fetish and my high arches appeal in their
filthy black patent stiletto heels i get bored during foreplay
stare at the unwashed jeans on the floor the smoke stained
paintwork the sex pistols poster that is on every wall of every
boy in every band in every white city every morning the reel
to reel soundscape of the third bus home sixth bus to work
dishwasher knife in hand scripted good mornings double
shot lattes for double breasted suits they were boys in bands
once too now second life mortgage marriage measuring up
making do i mend them with a smile clock off scribe copy
ignore the bassist save something for tomorrow sit out the
first song

magnetised

snakes of sweat send signals along spines separated by sounds of doubt sent down along the years all those years spent scurrying out of sight around corners stolen time and crowded rooms hid our hand holding hurried glances will it be like this forever for another eighteen years send me some kind of sign that only my soul can decipher save the discussion for another day bound by secrets you are so very fucking perfectly flawed and never ever ever false find me here when you least expect it always making me laugh wantonly you're a fuckstress and sometimes you just can't be fadged but nevertheless you seem to choose me even in the wake of all those sports model perfect opportunities that present themselves relentlessly you still choose to sit with me saving each second of tenderness and toothy grins and you're the only head i can stand to have against my shoulder all the others are just too heavy too submissive too dependent too demanding you hold me without fear of being broken and so i guess this is what trust feels like and maybe i've not been patient enough before never stuck it out like this before do you see the way we always come back to one another do you see how my feet always find your street even in the dark even in the rain even in the mirage heat of highest summer and do you see that you've been pulling me to you for eighteen years do you see that do you see how you save the best jokes for me how you can't wait to feed me tender sweetmeats and bracing coffee and cool my scars with frosted icy glass do you see that i can only hope that it never wavers this easy affection i heard a new queer term called mesh which makes room for the type of love that defies categorisation is that us is that us is that us perhaps perhaps we are just too hurt and cannot be tempted to fall into the abyss of neurosis that so easily accompanies such conventional affairs sold to us as the ultimate peak of status we were never meant to make that dream come true i can't be fenced in by white pickets and ticky tacky and neither can you you would drown in domesticity it would rob you of your light and even though it breaks our mothers hearts we will never make two point three cherubs with inky ringlets rosy cheeks and hands fit for concert hall musicians i want to be suspended in the moment you first looked at me with those electric lashes blurring your vision just enough so you could see the future i was living into and i want to hear you telling your brother about how smart i am again even if it was simply a riposte to him asking if you were dating me because we never know how to respond to that question it's never quite a no is it never quite a yes either even though our faces flush and our arms are driven together as if magnetised by destiny so what can we do do we go on paving the city streets with our desire mapping routes of connection endlessly a fractal pattern that leads only to each other even when it is interrupted by passing distractions shaped like lust disguised as passion but revealed to be violence at the sticking point sending us inevitably back to one another parched lonely hurting you always make me smile when i want to die always lift me out of that space under the bed too scared to come out because there's knives out there and my wrists are simply aching aching for the blade begging for sweetest oblivion you always remind me that friendship is a salve and that i have lived through so much worse so one cup of coffee with you is all it takes to bring me back to me and i can only hope i've done the same for you you say nobody can pronounce your name but that's not true is it your family can and your mother makes the best breakfast this side of the city and she doesn't bat an eyelid because we're mates and she phones the landline because who else would phone the landline and i miss our twenties do you remember how free we were always

rolling in up to the teeth with vodka stripping off and taking
snapshots of our perfect fucking skin wearing nothing but
a top hat or laughing until we cried in the wee hours on the
stupid bloody sofa-bed your cherry entrusted to me to devour
tenderly and you held me then much as you do now i think
you're the only lover i've ever had who doesn't despise me
so that must be why i cannot let you go so if we stay like this
this will be paradise i wouldn't change a thing about you i
miss our fifties when we will go on adventures because we
can finally afford to when we will laugh with our precious
friends around tables groaning with baking and reflect on
life's lessons learnt the hard way we will eventually wake up
with one another not all the time but from time to time and
time will hold us to our promises and you will still be whisk-
ing me away into the dark for kisses when we're way beyond
such childishness waste away with me by the ocean slake my
thirst and i'll feed you for a hundred years face the dark days
and the sleepless nights and the utter utter horror of it all
let's not be lonesome let's be daring and trick our frightened
palms into touching something tangible let's be fools for
once twice thrice i have confessed to you all of my sins this
cursed tongue and this demon flesh are wholly mine when
in your arms but might you bless me with your sanctuary
of company might you take my busy mind and quiet it with
your musician's fingers might you take a chance on this fire

Wasabi

Manners maketh man
Total control with a kiss
Chaos after lunch
Midwinter craving
Forgetting with someone new
Skin under my teeth
Kinbaku dreaming
Colour me in reflection
Make a cage of hope
To be bound to me
Spark a story in my gut
Wasabi flavoured
Thrill of the unknown
A strange mouth ripe for tasting
Blades beneath the tongue
Just one more pathway
One more knot and I am spent
Iridescent joy
Polyrhythmic pulse
Travelling unmapped desires
Strike a new backbeat

for the love of joni

under my skin
like that piercing tangerine ink
that stings more than the other colours
you are a bright painful honesty
showing me myself
and i can almost stand it
now that the years have
done their work on me
and you are still around

those little princes

they can get high and fall into the world
they can get bored and go and break a girl
little princes leave bruises
just because they can
they can get drunk and let their demons go
they can get lost and land a perfect blow
little princes leave bruises
to show that they're a man

Woman/Interrupted

This body writes away worries, expelling them like garbage, but they keep on coming back. Self-regenerating parasites feed off the flesh, figuring out how to trick the system and survive. A lifelong war waged on wellbeing. Surrender is never an option, even though oblivion is devilishly attractive, seductive. Come to me and see the light and suffer no more. Little girl blue. Little girl used. Little girl bruised by too-big-fingers finding too-small-spaces. You'd never know just from looking. You'd never guess she's tainted. You'd never ask, either.

Rise

We break out of the boxes
They built for us
And they burn us down
Blame us for being
Flame resistant
Build us new boxes
That are harder to break
But we keep on
Breaking
Burning
Resisting
Rising

Straya

this country breeds
scared, angry boys
blinded by their own
privilege
most of them learn
their way away
from the club, but
the rest, oh
the rest, they shout
over us, they
raise their fists, and
their firearms, and
if we continue to
disagree, well
that's when the
children die, the
women are raped
that's when the
hope is spread
so damn thin
we can't see
a way through
that's when we
want it all
to be
over

Dead Reckoning

Blue collar north
Welcomes collarless east
Prodigal daughter home
And I'm still
Younger than her
Even though she's
Forever in stasis
Trapped under tracks
And I'm still
Walking her path
To the station
And the streets have a rhythm
Red brick, blonde brick
Red brick, blonde brick
Blonde brick, red brick
Basket range
And I'm still looking
For her footprints
In the scrub
Still catch myself
Checking for her shadow
In the blue collar north

SapphoClique

Gold star
Dykecycle loyalty card
Just collect nine stamps
And your tenth fuck is free
But if you've ever
Kissed a boy
You're not allowed
In the club
You can watch from
The sidelines
But you'll never be
One of us

Danger/Dacryphilia

Mind so sharp
She cuts my eyes
And I leak
A sacrifice for her
Teeth so clever
She cracks my skull
And I bleed
A ballad for her

caught up

i've reached the sticking point when it comes to you and
how much space you take up in my everyday the day to day
the down to the millisecond split for the winner of this
marathon of magic make it stop make it stop make it stop see
now that i know the urgency and the agony of wanting i can
only hold onto hope that you do too too risky to say it out
loud but you have always read between my lines so finally it
is time to undo the code and flick the kill switch three two
one one more hint and i will rupture into pieces too bent to
be put back together again again i find my centre screams
for only you you are the drift net and i am yesterday's jetsam
ready to be gathered when it comes to you i've reached the
sticking point

# of passions and
obsessions

I sit empty, thirsting for words
grey phone calls sing
string of hearts snag curls
and all manner of flesh
gone wanting

brown bricks balance
around a place for a fire
heart/hearth
eclipsed by love and water gently rising
so that every light
gets scooped up
to nestle in an upside-down umbrella
like cherries in a floating bowl

I rush
but I need to be careful, or at least
soft with attention
open wide feeling
tucked into the fabric
weaving and unspinning the cocoon
simultaneously:
a butterfly delphinium
quivering along the stem

(focus)
by Lily Roberts

the ocean is the colour of God singing
God inside the water with white sea foam and
crystals of light
spearfishing the blurry deep

she is married to electricity
suffused with Love
that's love with a capital L
reaching like the root systems of mangroves
spread out, search, seek or sumptuous smirk
shirk the dark carpet underwater, dead black silt
that rises to become the sandcastle moats of children
they squeal alongside raucous claps of thunder
that roll in with the feral tide

pebbles dash the shoreline like a grazed knee scabs over
curlicues of water reach out
asking for one secret at a time
to collect, to take back
to the deep green hive
where the true sound of the ocean is silence
a suffocating shroud spread softly out
nine thousand fathoms down
deep sea mist
sirens calling, crawling downwards
to the surface
swimming upwards in waves
to alight upon the ocean floor
light refracting through endless green
mirrors in the making and the sea forever
a window

beneath them
the octopus keeps itself safe, its three hearts
beating in tandem inside the quiet
amphitheatre dark

(the ocean is the colour)
by Lily Roberts

Plant parent
by Dante DeBono

I have a keyring I bought a few years ago that proclaimed me a 'proud plant parent'. I'm an amateur horticulturalist, with a decent collection of pots scattered throughout my house: bedroom, lounge room, bathroom, and kitchen. Not to mention outside in the garden. I have pothos climbing up the walls and a fiddle-leaf fig tree that's over a metre tall. I wake up in the mornings to a line of avocado trees, still babies in my eyes, that I've managed to grow from seeds. I look forward to planting them one day, and in a decade's time maybe they will fruit. My elephant ear always has at least three leaves, waiting near the front door to welcome me home each day. I have a thriving parlor palm going on seven years and a brand-new rubber tree that will grow six times its size with the right care. And I intend to give it just that. I always do. But I'd have to say my specialty is succulents. I enjoy their crazy shapes and strange textures, and the way they can propagate themselves through dropped leaves, birthing miniature versions of the larger plants in an admirable show of resilience. Cuttings can be placed in fresh pots, and will happily establish a new root system until they stand on their own, reaching for the warmth of the sun. Succulents do that. They stretch out to the light, growing tall and leaning over, scattering leaves further apart along their stems to maximise exposure. And they can take more than most plants. They're as content in the desert as they are on my windowsill. They're hearty that way. In fact, overwatering is a death sentence. They won't stand it. But when their soil is dry, I give them a small drink and they thank me by continuing to grow. We sit in my backyard, a companionable silence between us as we bask in the warm light together, listening to the swaying of great, towering gumtrees in the valley beyond the fence, content. I've never had many issues with succulents when compared to other plants. Instead, I get to play around. I cultivate an array of varieties in a fancy, expensive pot from one of those hipster stores that gets put on a shelf like a display piece, living art. I care for a string of pearls cluster, strands pouring over the edges of a gravy boat like a waterfall, reminding me of my aunt who loves an unconventional planter. I experiment with the textures of cacti using careful touches, soft enough to avoid being pricked on their spikes, but I could never judge them if I were to nick a fingertip. I swap around the pot placements outside so I don't scorch the leaves in the heat of summer, because while it won't kill them, it is unsightly and I'm nothing if not a doting guardian. I do this again and again, constantly for years. It becomes a routine. I water on Wednesdays. I buy a moisture meter and pierce the topsoil with its metal prongs to see if it's finished drying or if it gets another week. I repot the plants who outgrow their homes, have dirt lodged under my nails for the rest of the day, softly emanating the scent of raw earth from when I gently massaged their roots to loosen the tangles so they'd be ready to stretch out in a bigger space. At least they can. Not me. Because there comes a time when we're locked in our homes, told to stay there. When we can't reach out and explore new horizons. They say it's the safest option, that we need to do it for the sake of more than ourselves. My grand plans for the year are foiled by an invisible threat that permeates the air all over the world. Nowhere is safe. Except home, hopefully. Home, where I spend months on end, not stepping past the perimeters of my fence. The paranoia seeps in like spores of mould, too fearful of infection to risk it. I avoid other people, avoid hands and hugs. Connections are strained, and conversations had through computer screens are not able to compare to those in person. There's no end in sight, an indefinite hiatus on life. It's just me and the plants I tend to. As stagnant as I feel, they continue to flourish throughout. I maintain my beloved title of 'proud plant parent', and keep my suburban jungle thriving. It gets me through the worst of the pandemic.

Smashed Avo on Toast
by Dante DeBono

A breakfast staple in Sarah's house had always been vegemite and avocado on toast. She had been eating it since she was a kid and still had it most mornings. It was a comfort food at this point. Just a standard pairing of salty carbs and not-really-a-fruit-but-classified-as-a-fruit-who-cares-it's-delicious. So…

'Why do I feel guilty?' Sarah asked.

Michael looked up from his phone to give her a confused look. 'What do you mean?'

'I feel guilty,' she repeated. 'It's stupid, I know, but come on. Smashed avo?'

'Oh my—' Michael huffed, eyes rolling. 'Don't be dumb.'

'But that's what I'm saying! It *is* dumb. I'm acknowledging how dumb it is that I, a millennial woman, feel guilty for ordering smashed avo on toast at brunch.'

'Okay, geez. Why don't you take a sip of your latte and calm down, huh?'

Unimpressed, Sarah pursed her lips. 'But aren't you mad?'

'About?'

Sarah gave up trying to articulate herself. It was probably stupid, anyway. Just the eventual culmination of seeing too many clickbait headlines about industries her generation had killed and why she couldn't afford a house because of her Netflix subscription. That's all it was. Somewhere along the line, eating avocado on toast became a symbol of failed adulthood or something and Sarah had simply internalised this concept.

She took a sip of her latte and tried to calm down.

Who cares that it cost seven dollars?

Sarah, apparently.

'That didn't help,' she admitted, staring pleadingly at Michael.

'You know, I don't think a boozy brunch is the place to unpack your existential crisis.'

'You're the only one drinking.'

'Yes, because I love myself,' Michael replied, taking a pointed sip of his mimosa.

And maybe that was the crux of it. Michael was the type of person who never had an issue treating himself to something frivolous for no better reason than he wanted to. He lived the life he chose, even if it didn't make sense to most people. His career was non-existent, earning money doing random odd jobs. This week he was walking dogs, last week he'd been a barista, and last month a roadie to some indie band Sarah had never heard of. He fluctuated between couch surfing and six-month rental leases, never wanting to be tied down. If he wanted to get drunk at brunch, he never hesitated.

Then there was Sarah, stressing about her seven-dollar latte that would inevitably come back to bite her because she was—yet to be diagnosed—lactose intolerant but didn't want to fork out another four dollars for soy milk, because she needed those four dollars for groceries if she planned on eating this week. Not to mention—

'Smashed avo on sour-dough toast with poached eggs,' the waitress announced.

Michael gestured in Sarah's direction, and it was set down on the table in front of her.

'And the sweet waffles with fruit compote and a side of bacon. Enjoy!'

Sarah looked across at the loaded plate Michael was already messing with, humming excitedly as he slathered syrupy strawberries on his choc-chip waffles. It was so different from her minimalist meal.

But she loved avocado on toast. It reminded her of her childhood and her mum. It was filling and yummy and healthy enough as far as breakfast foods go. And you know what? It was the cheapest thing on the menu.

With her knife held delicately in her right hand, Sarah split open an egg and watched the yolk ooze out to coat the mountain of avocado in molten gold.

The first bite was satisfying.

She tried not to feel guilty.

If Only Fences Kept Us Apart
by Belinda Lees

Positives in buying a house:

- *I will not be financially supporting the landlord Adaway's environmental destruction through paying rent while he paints and re-carpets the house.*
- *No more time wasted preparing spreadsheets to demonstrate to Adaway his wastefulness and environmental impact.*
- *Paying a mortgage rather than rent to Adaway.*
- *Be free from the ridiculous Adaway once and for all.*
- *I must buy a house!*

*

One of the things I appreciated when buying this home was that it wouldn't need painting for many years. I don't like to think about the environmental impact of painting. All those chemicals down the drains. Similarly, the harsh cleaning chemicals required when called upon for constant and impromptu rental inspections. I always think, *where does it all go?* It's the sort of thing that keeps me up at night. Not to mention recycling the empty cleaning bottles. It's one of the reasons I hardly drink from bottles! There's no household pick-up of glass in my town, so you have to take it all to the collection point. Petrol is consumed by taking bottles to the collection point. So, you can see that one's desire for a little mind-relaxing tipple rapidly cascades into an unforgivable, self-indulgent, environmental debt. Just like painting a property.

It's one of the reasons I left the house I was renting. I couldn't abide, nay, endorse the landlord's plans for new paint and new carpet through the payment of my monthly rent.

'Over my dead body,' I said.

'Now that you come to mention it,' he grumbled.

Some people can't handle adult conversations without resorting to sarcastic rebuttals, whereas I've always prided myself on direct communication. As my best friend Tony says: 'You're like a dog with a bone until you get your point across, and you know how to succeed even if it kills you.' So it had been with the landlord Adaway. He would suggest some manner of reckless and unnecessary renovation and I would launch a well-reasoned and well-planned case for leaving nature to its own devices. To think of the sleepless nights I spent preparing spreadsheets just to politely challenge that twit. That and the headaches.

I also felt it was time I stopped lining someone else's pockets when I could be paying off my own mortgage. As the years wore on, I simply couldn't stomach piling cash onto the environmental maniac that is Adaway. I was enabling him in his contribution to the destruction of the planet.

Another element I sought out was a small yard which would mean less mowing and polluting fewer fumes into the atmosphere, and no noxious weed and pest killers and the like. Adaway was a lawnmowing fiend. Every week, regardless of the season, he would mow the damn lawn, as per his ridiculous clause in the lease. When my verbal protests failed, I took to heaving my outdoor setting all over the yard as a barrier, often while he was mowing! Nothing deterred that obsessive mower.

My house also has a lovely gumtree which attracts native birds: wattle birds, magpies, and lorikeets. On the downside, a rail line runs behind the house which exacerbates my tendency toward insomnia. Tony, always the pragmatist, said that before long I wouldn't even notice the train and I'd be sleeping like a baby.

'Which baby?' I demanded to know. Daisy, my sister's infant, is renowned neighbourhood-wide for her nocturnal screaming sessions. Don't even get me started on the environmental impact of babies! Snapshots of Daisy make Munch's 'The Scream' look like an indolent yawn.

I often wonder, *isn't everyone experiencing sleeplessness with the state of the world these days?* Maybe Daisy is precocious for her age and is already attuned to the zeitgeist. I try to self-soothe by reminding myself that I'm doing my best. I'm contributing my bit on my tiny square of Earth. *Separate your recycling items into cardboard, plastics, glass, and soft plastics, Celia, and all will be well with the world.*

I guess what I'm actually saying is I'm not an environmental saint, but I do believe there's no excuse for a wanton disregard of the rules. So, I was despairing when, on the first recycling day in my new home, I discovered that a neighbour had filled my recycling bin with general refuse. I happened upon the mayhem when I opened the bin to sneak in a milk carton before collection. There I found five cheesy pizza boxes, a split open plastic bag spilling old cat litter, and another plastic bag bursting with soiled nappies. The putrefying stench propelled me backward. It didn't take a detective to figure out who was to blame. One quick glance to the right revealed the culprit whose own recycling bin was bursting with household refuse.

What was intended to be a quick dash to the bin in my dressing gown turned into a race down the road and a spontaneous introduction to the neighbourhood. I invest a lot of importance in first impressions and I would have preferred not to have the neighbours see me in this state of informality. With no time to spare, however, carrying greasy

pizza boxes under one arm and the bags in the other hand,
I ran down the road to see if anyone had space in their bin.

Three houses down I found a bin with potential, so I
knocked on the door. I rang the bell.

'Yes?' he said, an older man in a pastel blue tracksuit.

'Hi. I'm Celia. I notice you have space in your bin. Would
you mind if I placed my neighbour's garbage in there for
pickup?'

'No, I'm sorry.'

The garbage truck rounded the corner.

'Please? It's my neighbour's. She snuck it into my recycling
bin. There's the truck.'

At that moment, cat dirt escaped from the split in the bag
and landed on his neat porch. He looked from the faeces to
the litter sprinkling out of the bag to the browning nappy-
filled bag, and then to me.

'No.' He cringed. 'I had the bin cleaned last week.'

'But it will barely touch the sides. There's the truck!'

He closed the door.

I ran to the next neighbour's bin. It was full.

Perhaps, I thought, *I could reason with the truck driver.*
He could empty a bin, then I could place the rubbish back
in that bin, then he could empty it again.

The driver was emptying my bin when I knocked on his
door.

'Hello!' I shouted. 'Please, I have this extra garbage.'

He wound down his window.

'I only collect from bins.'

'Yes, I'll put it back in my bin and you can empty it again.'

He shook his head in that wearied manner of the bored
self-important. 'No. There are limits. One bin per household.'

'But it's not my garbage, it's my neighbour's.'

'One bin per household!'

He drove to the next bin.

❋

I do enjoy sipping on an alcoholic beverage on special celebrations, such as graduations, birthdays, or when a particularly annoying colleague announces their resignation, but that night I opened a bottle of Shiraz to keep the rage at bay. Perhaps it was the wine, maybe the stress, or maybe the bloody trains, but I barely slept. The inner tempest brewed and developed into a category three cyclone.

At 3.05am I turned on the light and grabbed a notebook and pen from my side table. I detailed each of the issues, teasing them out one at a time:

- *Contamination of recycling.*
- *Confrontation with new neighbour. If I don't speak now, this transgression will continue forever. Remember, direct adult communication.*
- *Her filthy waste in my bin. It is so disgusting, just to think about it.*
- *What to do with her waste?*
- *I must create a spreadsheet to record her environmental impact and my counteractions. I must do this immediately.*

❋

Tony wasn't thrilled to fill his boot with my neighbour's garbage and couldn't see why I wouldn't just leave it in my own bin for the week, but as lifelong besties, sometimes you just have to offer the benefit of the doubt. Also, Tony knows that if my little compulsions aren't soothed and sated in the early stages, then I tend to become bedevilled by them.

'I'm sorry, Tony, but it's stomach-churning! I've already endured one sleepless night fixated on that multitude of festering germs. I will not spend another. To the council's dump!'

I wasn't thrilled about paying fifty dollars to deposit my neighbour's waste in landfill, either. I would enter it into my spreadsheet when I got home.

On the way back, we stopped at the council offices where I picked up a collection of recycling brochures.

I waited until it was dark and then popped them into ten neighbours' letterboxes. This way she wouldn't feel targeted. I knew it was an inadequate measure, but if my work as a data processor has taught me anything, it's the importance of following process.

✳

The next fortnight, when the recycling bin was due to be emptied, I waited until the morning to wheel it onto the curb. No sooner had I poured myself a coffee than I saw my neighbour stuffing bags of rubbish into my general waste bin and my recycling bin.

I confronted the woman right there, fresh from the crime.

'Ah, hello. Hello there. Yes, hi. I'm Celia. Um, what—what do you think you're doing?'

I prefer not to be judgemental, but just by looking at her, I could see she was the kind of person who'd stuff her garbage into another person's recycling bin. Perhaps it was the permanent sneer, or the cigarette stuck to her bottom lip.

'You had space,' she said.

'Well, ah, firstly... Firstly, it's polite to ask before you place your garbage into another person's bin, and secondly, you're putting rubbish into the recycling bin. You're contaminating my recycling.'

She looked me down and then looked me up and then turned on her heels and made for her house.

'Where are you going? You can't leave your garbage in my recycling bin. Again!'

The door slammed.

The garbage truck rounded the corner.

'Come back out here at once!'

She was turning out to be just as obstinate as Adaway. If it wasn't maniacal lawnmowing, it was self-centred contamination of the recycling.

Damn, damn, and double damn!

I retrieved her garbage from my recycling bin. I'm not proud of my next move, since I'm not a particularly vindictive person, but you tell me what else I could have done! I traipsed her garbage over to her yard and then dropped it over the fence. After all, it was her belongings. I merely returned the objects to their rightful owner. I was simply following the rules.

I certainly did not anticipate finding that same garbage at my front door when I arrived home from a day at the office. As I said, I'm not a drinker but a little wine was required to quell the inner storm.

Later, at 2.32 in the morning, I sought to disentangle my wrath through the application of pen to paper:

- *I could be the bigger person and put the garbage in my empty bin, impacting on my own capacity for garbage the following week. Though, let's face it, I rarely fill the bin above halfway.*
- *I don't want **her filthy garbage** in my bin, festering for a week before pick-up.*
- *I don't want her to think she can bully me into this co-dependent garbage-enabling relationship.*
- *She needs to know that she can't contaminate recycling.*
- *She needs to know that she can't just pile her disgusting germ-infested junk on top of my junk.*
- *I hate her junk. I really hate it.*
- *Her junk must go!*

Tony declined to drive me to the council dump because he'd just had his car detailed and wasn't going to have my, 'neighbour's bloody trash stinking the joint up again'. By the time I paid for the taxi and the refuse fee, I was seventy dollars worse off. It was later recorded on my spreadsheet.

The next fortnight passed without incident because I did not put out my recycling bin for collection. *Two can play at this game*, I chuckled to myself. Deep down, however, I knew that in the long game, the planet was losing. If it wasn't my bin, it was someone else's.

Meanwhile, the doctor was reluctant to prescribe sleeping pills because in her mind, there was a solution to the problem that didn't require medical intervention.

'You don't understand,' I said. 'This person is destroying the planet singlehandedly. Every fortnight she contaminates the recycling with trash. Who knows how long she's been doing this. Think of all the truckloads of waste that she has created through her selfish overconsumption. Think of the oceans, suffocating because of her laziness and grotesque lifestyle. Imagine if you did the sums on this!'

'Put it out of your mind,' she said in a soppy, patronising tone.

'I can't put it out of my mind. It's literally all I can think of. I feel responsible. She's my neighbour.'

'Have you complained to the council?'

✳

The receptionist at the council thanked me for my concern and assured me that they would deal with it, but when recycling day arrived and I wheeled out my bins just before the predicted truck arrival time, I felt that I couldn't leave my bins unattended, because deep down I knew nothing had changed. I busied myself with some weeding of the nature strip while waiting and I noticed that her recycling bin was, again, stuffed to the point of regurgitating with garbage bags.

'Thought you'd get me in trouble, did you?'

I flinched. She was behind me, hands on hips, cigarette dangling from her mouth.

'You're not very neighbourly, are you? Not used to sharing, I suppose. Me? I have to look after my daughter's kids, my other daughters' kids, and I like to be sociable, you know. All of that creates a bit more garbage than a person who just looks after themself. That's what you've got to factor in. So, if you've got extra space, then what harm is it? I'm catering for an army over here while you're all alone.'

Ash dropped off the end of the cigarette onto my freshly weeded nature strip.

I wanted to mention the stream of cars that parked in front of my house, the constant racket of children and music and swearing, the never-ending cigarette pollution that wove and wafted its way into my yard and up my nostrils, the cat that defecated under my drought-resistant Roundleaf Correa, but I didn't, because although it was all mind-blowingly annoying, it was not the issue at hand, which was the planet. But first: a small victory. A single bin.

'One bin per household. There are limits,' I said. 'But the real issue is recycling.'

I tried to dissipate the ash with my foot.

She chuckled. The garbage truck rounded the corner.

'Keeping watch, are you? Making sure I don't use your recycling bin?'

'I'm sure I can trust you to do the right thing,' I said, 'by the planet.'

'Shouldn't you be getting off to work?'

'What concern is it of yours?'

'I can bring your bins in for you, if you like.'

'Thank you, but no, that's all right.'

'Just being neighbourly.'

Had I not taken the day off work to guard my recycling bin, I would not have witnessed my neighbour carrying two garbage bags down the road, peeking inside every recycling bin until she found space to stuff them. She brushed her hands against one another in a self-satisfied gesture. Then she strutted back past me and into her house, sneering.

Of course, I dashed down the road and retrieved them, but I waited until the recycling truck had passed before I dropped her rubbish bags over her front fence.

Later, when I collected the mail, I discovered my lawn strewn with garbage. The thing that appalled me most was that actual garbage was intermingled with recyclables. There had been no attempt to separate the items. I found a laundry detergent bottle, ice cream containers, cardboard packaging intermingled with babies' diapers, and a broken bag of filthy cat litter, that was now embedded in my lawn. Not to mention all the soft plastics that could be returned to the supermarket, or the bottles that could be delivered to the collection point.

*

- *Bevs out of control thinks shes so clever sneaking down road to put her garbage in nonsusspectating peoples bins and is just sneakily destroying the planet this way so bad*
- *Bev is an environmental terrorist she is*
- *No she **really** is really*
- *Bev must be bloody **educated***

*

After lunch, I made my way next door.

She jostled a grizzling child on her hip, while a cigarette hung from her mouth.

'What is it? I'm busy.'

'I'd like to show you, you, how you can separate your trash into recycling. I've itemised your rubbish-h h-here on this list.'

'You've been drinking.'

'Anyway, we're talking about your rubbish-ish, and how you can contribute to a healthier planet by separating your items appropriately.'

'I don't care.'

'Don't care? 'Bout the planet?'

'No. I don't care. Now, I'm busy.'

She closed the door in my face.

I took a taxi to the council dump for the trash, then the supermarket to deposit the soft plastics, then the collection point for the bottles. I picked up another couple of bottles of Shiraz at the bottle shop, rounding the day's expenditure up to an even hundred dollars. It was straight to the spreadsheet with those receipts!

I don't know if it was the wine or the rage, but I couldn't sleep at all that night. I'm not a petty person, but, I thought, *if I can't sleep, I may as well put my energy into process.* My spreadsheet calculations, which took me all of six hours and thirty-nine minutes to complete, proved that I am not petty, and that in fact, it is she who is a major culprit in destroying the planet. Basically, when all the sums are completed and you look in the cold harsh light of morning at her lifelong contribution to climate change, well, one wonders how viable she is, as an individual specimen of a species.

I'm a believer in balance. If it were possible for me to curtail my own habits to such a degree that I could meaningfully offset her waste, I would do it, but it's simply not possible. It would take three people, or more.

In an attempt to quell the inner frenzy, I developed a meditation that morning based on what astronauts say about being in outer space. They say that once you've seen the planet from afar, you can never think of life in the same way. The little things just don't matter anymore. So, I imagined seeing the planet from afar. I inhaled and allowed my mind to float like a helium balloon, up, up, up. I inhaled and felt my torso swaying side to side as my mind elevated to an intergalactic dimension. Up, up, up. *Don't look down,* I chanted, *don't look down, until you're in outer space*! Up, up, up. But something was anchoring me to my town. Don't look down! But look I must, and did, and like a spy movie satellite, my mind homed in on my neighbourhood, streets sharpened into focus, my inner-eye vision recalculated and recalibrated, and then, yes, there in hyperreality was Bev's house. A big black spot! Her environmental impact was so vast that it was visible from outer space, albeit through the use of my inner-eye hyperreality satellite.

I must emphasise that, upon reflection, I'm not proud of my thinking, and I'm not sure whether it was the cumulative effect of insomnia, or the dehydration from the wine, but my mind developed a fantasy. I'm sitting in Tony's car, watching, waiting for the moment she opens the lid on my recycling bin, then lightning fast, I reverse, and save the planet. *Nature is harsh*, I reasoned. *Nature is decisive.* If something is out of balance, nature will find a way to correct it. Sometimes, nature needs a hand. I am nothing if not an ally of nature.

'But I don't understand,' Tony said. 'What is the point of leaving my car in your driveway?'

'It's not something I can express in words,' I said. 'And can you give me your keys?'

'You don't have a licence.'

'Just until tomorrow morning. I'll pay for your taxi home and back. And for any other expenses incurred.'

Tony folded his arms. 'Is this something to do with your neighbour's rubbish?'

'I'm just considering the big picture, Tony.'

'You look like you haven't slept for a month, and you smell like a brewery. And, why aren't you at work?' He pointed a finger in my direction. 'What do you mean *other expenses*?'

'You are very much the inquisitor, aren't you, Tony?'

'No. I won't do it.'

'What happened to giving each other the benefit of the doubt?'

Tony shook his head. 'I will take you to the doctor, Cel. Have a shower and get dressed.'

'That lazy nature-hater. No, thank you.'

Apparently, I'd forgotten to call in sick to work. Arguing with Tony had distracted me from my phone, so I'd missed HR's calls. HR pulled up out the front just as Tony was trying to usher me back inside.

'Damn it! What's she doing here?' I said.

'I'll sort it.'

Tony shoved me inside, then closed the door behind me. He delivered a series of plot points including food poisoning, dehydration, and delirium. 'A trip to the hospital is imminent,' he said.

Once HR had left, Tony insisted on taking me to the doctor.

'You just don't look right,' he said.

'There is only one thing I need, Tony, and that is an assurance that she—' I pointed towards next door's. '—will stop contaminating the recycling.'

'Are you crying?'

'Of course I'm bloody crying, Tony!'

'Perhaps you should stay with me for a while, until this whole thing blows over.'

I shook my head. Tony clearly didn't get it. This 'thing' as he so dismissively put it, was never going to 'blow over'.

Not while she produced garbage, and for as long as she lived, she would produce garbage. She's in her fifties. She had decades of garbage left to generate, decades left to destroy the planet. *But*, I wondered, *does the planet have decades left to cop this abuse*?

I wiped my cheeks.

'Just a little exhausted,' I said. 'A good sleep is all I need.'

Tony nodded. 'Have a rest, Cel, and I'll call you this afternoon.'

'The car, Tony?'

He shook his head. I try to be magnanimous, but I caught myself sneering at Tony.

I would show Tony. One day I would get a car of my own and then I would save the planet. Or at least rid the world of one less impediment to its existence. In the meantime, however, I would have to take my neighbour's recycling into my own hands.

I waited until dark. I wheeled her bins into my yard and then tipped her garbage onto my lawn. *How to proceed*, I wondered. *Methodically, Celia. Glass to the right. Soft plastics to the left. Hard plastics at the top. Cardboard and papers down below.* Apart from the stench, it was almost hypnotic. Meditative even. It only took me two hours to rearrange it into categories. I then wheeled her bins back out to the curb, freshly organised.

I knocked on her door.

'It's you. What do you want?'

I tried to point to the bins, but I couldn't lift my arm.

'Thath srange,' I said, 'can' liff m'arm.'

'What's wrong with your face?'

'Wassat?'

'Your face. Are you having a stroke?'

'Throke?'

'Come in and sit down. I'll call an ambulance.'

'Need m'purth. Need t'lockup.'

✳

I try not to think about her entering my house unattended in search of my bag. I try not to think of her inspecting the spreadsheet of calculations about her lifetime's consumption that was lying next to my bag. Because I'm not the kind of person who holds a grudge. Every fortnight when she wheels out my recycling bin for collection, I try, instead, to focus on the neighbourly life-saving gesture of calling the ambulance. I try.

'Thanks, Bev, but you really don't have to. My friend Tony can do it.'

'Just being neighbourly.'

Meanwhile, Tony has stepped into the breach. When someone, a friend, a best friend, nonetheless, offers to help a person through a particularly rough patch in their life, 'no matter what it takes', I take that best friend at his word.

'Come and stay with me, Cel. I'll look after you until you're back on your feet.'

'There's only one thing I really need, Tony...'

'Don't say it, Cel. It'll be so much easier, so much better if you just come and stay with me. Forget about all of this. Forget about her.'

'You promised, Tony.'

Tony lowered his head in resignation.

He'll be here any minute to help with the sorting. I tell him to wait until it's dark so Bev can't see him. I tell him he needs to make sure that there's no glass in the bags, and no soft plastics, and if there are, he needs to separate them out and we'll drive them to the supermarket and collection point tomorrow, after we take the rubbish to the council dump. Unfortunately, there are three motorcycle riders staying at

Bev's now, so that means additional waste. I saw her sneaking down the road with numerous bags after she'd already crammed my bins full. As I explained to Tony, there's no point challenging Bev on this matter, firstly, because no one tells Bev anything, and secondly, Bev's house guests look like the kind of people who would pulverise Tony if he upset them. Poor Tony. It will be a long night finding and sorting all her waste. But sorting the waste is the neighbourly thing to do.

The thing I used to ask myself was how many Bevs are out there, contaminating the recycling every fortnight? And putting glass and soft plastics in with their waste? It kept me awake at night and spreadsheets only went so far toward scratching the itch. In the meantime, the rage brewed and because I'm not supposed to drink alcohol there was no way to quell the storm. For a while I contemplated moving again, but then Bev would still be Bev, and no doubt I would come across another Bev or another Adaway, or even perhaps a lawnmowing-fiend recycling-contaminator bundled into one cigarette-sucking body. So, I try, instead, to focus on the Bev that lives next door. Thank goodness for Tony and his promise to help me through my recovery, *no matter what it takes*. I can tell that the fortnightly recycling sorting is wearing thin, as are the jaunts to the council dump, the soft plastics recycling at the supermarket, and the glass collection point, but it's all part of my self-developed rehabilitative exercise program.

✳

Positives in staying here:

- *Bev's poor behaviour gives me additional exercise opportunities every fortnight.*
- *Bev's poor behaviour allows Tony and I to strengthen our friendship. I have to trust that Tony is exercising*

due diligence when collecting and sorting Bev's garbage.

- *Bev's poor behaviour allows Tony to selflessly contribute to the health of the planet, despite his personal wishes.*
- *Bev's poor behaviour keeps my data processing skills updated as I maintain spreadsheets on her.*
- *I dealt with Adaway for ten years, I can deal with Bev. Bev is here to stay, but so am I.*

into ruminations

the sound of crickets through the backdoor screen
little boy sneaks around the house at dawn

runs along the river, eyes set like blood in the vein
light refracting to colour a sunset
in a dream, a boat flies high
my tree captures/catches and the branches make a cradle
for the blue hull caught in one hand and the sails
unfurled with the other. I'll scream
to the wind, pull hard at the edges of the trees
force uncover
that which dwells at the centre, waits for me
in a pool of remembering
sing, hail the forest, come alive
instead of decaying under the carpet like
a flat piece of paper, wet from imagined snow

I need reminders:
lit matches, smell of sulphur
apricots, too hard or too soft
how tears feel on my face, like worlds above and below suffering
cigarette smoke
pomegranate seeds
and the six of hearts, repeating like a flat promise,
'You'll love. You'll love. You'll love.
You'll love. You'll love. You'll love.'

(mud)
by Lily Roberts

olive oil slick on the floor
violets and the sudden smell of pepper
the way the grater
dismantles the carrots
I am left with a pile of wet
stuff that clings:
this grief that's always
a step ahead of
or behind me
a shadow that moves with the
sun of his mood

(arbitrary)
by Lily Roberts

Landline/Lifeline
by Heather Briony McGinn

At 96 Yorktown Road, there sits a Bakelite landline in 1960s office green. Silverbeet sits in the sink, glossy, iron-rich. It rests in an ancient, third-hand colander, liberated from its earthly decorations, clay-threaded soil now winding a path through pipes to who knows where. Barefoot on the lino, each toe warming the surface and summoning the scent of yesterday's bleach. There are towels on the Hills Hoist. Semaphore via a washing line. This house is cradled by routine. First cup of tea barely minutes after dawn. Second cup of tea with breakfast. Third cup of tea after the breakfast dishes are done—this one is accompanied by biscuits. Fourth cup of tea with lunch. Fifth cup of tea after the lunch dishes are done. Afternoon tea with a sweetie. Proper tea—dinner—without a cup of tea but rather a beer. Sixth, and final, cup of tea—a substitute for dessert.

The greenhouse is always magical. Murky half-light, half-neon from the combination of salvaged panels of corrugated plastic panels and too-large leaves. Orchids are of paramount importance here. Ornamentals warrant their own house. Food crops take up the unguarded space of the backyard, bridging the distance between her shed and his. Poppa's house is tiny and reserved for gardening tools alone. Nanna's shed is bigger. A treasure trove of utility and making do. Endless stacks of tins of haberdashery supplies. Spare rations. An altar too, just in case. In cases upon cases. Just in case it happens again. 'It' could be anything. Any flavour of threat or danger or poverty that could be guarded against by careful planning. Forearmed in the face of a multitude of imagined forewarnings. Even though refrigerators are a thing now, we can be without one and be just fine.

At a moment's notice, we can return to a way of being that sustained us before. Before war. After war. Recovering, with fabric, food, and family. Rejuvenating, seed by seed, stitch by stitch, scone by scone. Ever ready. We are batteries, fully charged and dormant. When the crisis erupts, we will work. Industry is all we have ever known. Knowing is a new language. Doing is our way. Busy-ness. Business is a foreign land. Work is home. Home is work. Work isn't a punch card. It is everything, it is in our bones. It is bread and babies and bathtubs and bitumen plucked from broken skin on knee-caps, iodine stings, Band-Aids from the Band-Aid tin. All of this while the spinach drains and the silverside rests and the table is laid in time for the boys to tumble in. They hang up their work clothes and wash their hands and make sure the animals are fed. They check the letterbox and hand over their wages and wait for Nanna to hand back fifty cents for the gee-gees. The girls do their homework. Poppa completes the cryptic crossword and everyone knows what's for lunch tomorrow. Sandwiches in brown paper and the last of this week's cake. Yum. Always more to do.

Winters are heralded by the blossoming of the loquat tree. The first fruits fall two days before the start of spring, and are swiftly gathered into recycled ice cream containers, ready for jam and responsible for several sore tummies. Smooth stones at the centre of the soft flesh are thrown with impu-nity at endless cousins, even though we ought to have grown out of such games. We troop back inside at the first sign of sunset and set the table with a practised precision. Identical foreheads and hands. All the same as Nanna's. Proud Vikings, all. We eat quickly, economically, never pausing for a second longer than necessary. And the boys do the dishes while the girls gather the pets inside for the night. No dead birds on the doorstep for this household. So many limbs spill over armchairs that there's barely room for coffee mugs, a cosiness created from the limits of time and space. An abundance of dreams squeezes into one front room.

Spread across continents now, spaces seem too large and cold, always cold in comparison to those leaner days. Days pinched at the corners by budgets and punch-cards. Days left behind in the wake of free education and multiple births. How many sets of twins now? Three. No, four. Every portrait has its Gemini peeking around the frame. Eyes the same shape but different colours, running the spectrum of bleached slate to sinister emerald. Hemmed in by heavy eyelashes showing no sign of thinning with age. So far apart but so close in humour and the same photographs in the same arrangement. Never discussed but always watching, reminding us that the women never make the first cup of tea, because the women do everything else. The women's hands are paper dry from industry and worry, heavy with the flesh-memory of a Bakelite telephone. Ready to take the call and meet the challenge, whatever it may be.

Why did the koala cross the road?
by Dante DeBono

The car rumbles its way through shifting gears, trying to get up to speed, the black road rapidly disappearing beneath its wheels. Everything glows with the orange hue of streetlights, illuminating all four lanes of traffic and the late-night drivers just trying to get where they're going.

In the distance appears a shadow, small and roundish. Moving. Crawling its way across the dark asphalt at a gradual but determined pace. I slow, still uncertain what for, the break gradually easing downwards beneath my foot, rolling to an eventual stop.

My headlights reveal grey fur and rounded ears, clawed hands dropping at a steady pace as the koala crosses the road.

It seems wrong, the sight of it. For me, koalas are wild things with deep-rooted instincts and eucalyptus-tinged breath, not meant to be found in suburbia. Roads of crude oil, drilled and distilled into bitumen, filled with cars that spill out black exhaust. People and their houses that stand where trees once did, their lawns sprouting from foreign seeds and sharp-toothed pets brought here in much the same way. All of it is a threat to this native creature who seems to become rarer with each passing day.

I suppose the question isn't
> *Why did the koala cross the road?*

but,
> *Why is there a road he must cross?*

I drive on once my lane is free from wandering wildlife, the koala continuing on its way. I hope it gets where it's going.

Nostalgia
by Dante DeBono

I collect the dried petals of flowers picked last spring the way my grandmother hoards trinkets in her rundown house. When do you consider them pointless and throw them away? Are they ever not pointless to start with?

They crinkle and shatter beneath my fingers, delicate—all their life drained by the passing of days, strung up in my window. I pick up each of the fallen leaves as they release their hold on twig-like stems, smell long since faded to a musty memory along with once vibrant colours. But it feels wrong to deem them useless now. Haven't we all grown weary on occasion?

Unlike herbs or teas, they can't be consumed. They're not remedial. They don't taste nice. They can't offer warmth and comfort on a winter's day from the confines of a steaming mug. As I said, pointless. But still, I keep them all. There's a jar I put them in, the dried remnants of many a bouquet, but not really. Bouquet implies purpose and that's not what they have. They just are what they are, and I treasure them anyway. I've grown attached to the small tragedy of their existence. The way I can hold it in my hand.

I think of my grandmother's house again. The blending of inside with outside. Rusting furniture on the crowded porch. Dirt-covered floors littered with insects. Overgrown and wild. A lop-sided home sinking back into the land. The swaying gums surround it, seeming to creep closer with each year gone by. The thought pleases me.

I think of my jar of dried petals and leaves.

When they arrive, will the trees see my collection and spare me?

A (De)Lineation Interval

by Lyndal Hordacre Kobayashi

Three Poems in Black Lines

Poem 1.

ruminations

ruminating on green,
a creative linguist
watches images,
hurry away with words

into the banded malachite world they rush,
espying clouds circling the tips of majestic trees,
branches beckoning to distant realms
and prehistoric valleys,
condensing time

'come back,' she pants
and reaches
for the door of the sky parlour,
painted with emerald streaks
and layered with tiny reminiscent effervescing crystals

enticed by words' unexplainable wisdom,
the images return
but are stealthily disunited from their friends,
subjected
to the room beyond
the sky parlour's door

struck by the Gordian knot,
the linguist paints a picture,
words typed to explain

an unworded world...

the images scamper wildly
within the recesses of their space,
creeks expand
mountains swell
a tranquil sun encourages
the pop of delicate viridescent buds
unfurling green tendrils stretch
into the cracks,
yonder they move

downstairs, the words sit
immobile and glum
'where's my vision,' yells sight,
'*i* can't find it, can't feel a thing,' answers touch
'what?' asks sound
'no fragrances, sob,' reminisces scent
'not hungry,' harks taste

senses lost
words asunder

but through the gaps the popped buds grow
perception bounces forward
and lightly grabs the extending leaves,
the latch springs open

once together again
words and images embrace
enfolding, wrapping, merging
like magnets assimilating truth and fable
embroidering histories
for future stories to be told

Poem 1
braids together
and equally apart
my research of
words,
silences,
bodily senses,
concepts,
embodiment,
creativity,
and Merleau-Ponty's
'Phenomenology of Perception'.

what is a word?
a tactile thing,
a sensory object
or subject,
a scent,
a taste?

or a memory
from afar,
a whisp of smoke,
a cultural connection
with self?
how heavily laden
it is?

i turn inwards
to play,
watching

sensory experiences
make meanings
together.

what if
the word
becomes
a physical thing?
words become forms
but forms are no longer words
tantalising
what will it do?
how will it act?

this story
divides words from images.
together
they take journeys,
conjure up travels and discoveries
and explain their experiences,
but
their behaviour changes
when separated.
whilst detached,
images continue to flourish,
revelling in their time,
unconstrained,
creative,
curious,
childlike
and somewhat naïve.

however,
words are less fortunate

without images,
words lose their sensual experiences.
it is not until perception,
an interesting
connection maker,
bridges the separation,
recreating a relationship
between words
and images.

perception,
a creative force sourcing fun
always experimenting
absorbing
delivering
through
an image,
a prompt,
an association,
or remembered experience.

every creative process
challenges,
confronting
any notion of knowledge.

Poem 2.

gåsunger tårer (gosling's tears)

the world was verdant
fragrant and humming
but there was a grove
with withering plumules
sprouting briny tears
unable to nourish

but no one
bent down
to listen
to the voice
of tears
with crooked backs
and feeble legs
the distance
was too
far

do tears have voices?
i hear you ask
pay attention
i reply

listen

Poem 2
sits
in
a
space
where
the joy of rejuvenation
merges
with sadness

the disappearing green world
embodied in a blossoming twig,
growing as it is thwarted
by buds of tears

the image comes alive
as the hand draws it
where was it
before becoming?
the woman-made line
finds a disruption,
depicting nature
engulfed by briny sorrow

soft warm down
on the tips
of growing goslings' heads,
the fuzzy buds
warm my heart

but buds on branches

gulp without breath
forming the shape of tears
dripping with cool serous liquid
unable to sustain
the life
of the sapling
it bleeds from

wisdom should be nearby
boughs bending
together
to advise the sapling,
but the old
and blackened lines
no longer live,
having long ago
embodied
the sentiments of humans,
shedding tears
that drown all sorrows

interjection of a grub

Feeling Forming Feeling
by Dr Amelia Walker

Grub-like, I inch along
this black vine that could be and is
all colours, beyond colours,
shapes now curved,
now rigid, arcing to points
like leaves. I nibble,
coursing veins of evolution,
histories unknown,
yet inescapable in their here
and now-ness. Each bite
bursts sounds, sensations
of sobbing, laughter, teardrops
breath: I am breathing
this black vine,
as it breathes me,
breeds me, makes me
all I know and do not know.
Forming feeling,
feeling forming,
I inch along,
grub-like.

forming feeling forming
by Lyndal Hordacre Kobayashi

145

grub-like, I inch along,
my body imitating
this black line that could be and is
remembering
all colours beyond colours,
sensual tones balancing on
shapes, now curved,
now rigid, braced to support
diamond formed leaves. I nibble
through coursing veins of evolution,
hats and histories unknown,
yet inescapable in their here
and now-ness. each gossamer-thin bite
bursts sounds, sensations
of sobbing, laughter, heart-felt teardrops,
my breath: I am breathing
this black line
as it breathes me
bleeds me, makes me
all I know and do not know.
forming feeling,
feeling forming
I inch along
grub-like.

Poem 3.

ChanGinG GREEN

It would only have to be small,
a tiny root system clinGinG
to the shallow crevice between rocks,
a few leaves forminG,
pullinG in the Goodness
the sun freely dispenses,
Gravity somewhere distant,
knowinGly watchinG the moment,
ready to play aGainst
the upwards pull of the sun
where do the roots start and end?
they resemble the creepinG line of the Gap
they follow,
hollowinG out the space,
searchinG,
nimble,
as flexible
as a free form movement
of the letter 'G'
drawn

It would only have to be small,
the flickeR at the corner of heR lips
as she bRushes
the uneven bits
of heR newly cRopped fRinGe

away from her eyes,
Remembering the sound
of the scissors
as they beGan
the tRansfoRmation
she has been yeaRning foR,
watchinG heR paRtinG haiR
fall to the GRound
in little chunks of childhood days
wheRe choices
weRe neveR heR own
the lettuce GReen dRess
is left at home,
lying on heR bed,
flouncinG aGainst the bReeze,
tiny matchinG pointy shoes
on the flooR
undeRneath

It would only havE to bE small,
vibRations in the EaRth,
oR the fluttER of buttERfly winGs,
GRound movEmEnts
that GRow in volumE,
friEnds who link aRms,
trEEs silEntly connEctinG
bElow thE suRfacE,
unnoticEd,
unhEaRd,
unmEntionEd,
a GREEn tREE fRoG's
cRoak

It would only havE to bE small,
the sizE of a fly's GOGGlEd EyE
Glowing GREEn,
pausEd on a sticky lEaf
covEREd with translucEnt aphids
suckinG
thE plant's sap flowinG
from tREE to aphid
in a sinGlE stRaw likE
suck,
the GREEn blood
of the tREE
takEn into thE conE-shapEd
mouth of thE aphid,
the paRasitE,
the lifE
takER

It would oNly have to bE small,
aN EmbRyo makiNG
the tiNiEst sigNs
of RockiNG
as it shaREs
movEmENt
back aNd foRth,
back aNd foRth
back aNd foRth
tEmpo
a pEN follows the liNEs,
a sidEways c,
a RockiNG chaiR,
half-mooNs
aNd a ChRistmas tREE,
who would havE
thouGht?

It would oNly havE to bE small,
GREEN WRittEN iN a maRGiN
of a GRass staiNEd,
GRubby wEll-REad book,
huRlEd out to sEa
likE pEbblEs with thEiR shiNy suRfacEs,
cRashiNG toGEthER over millENNia
GREEN fiNds its way,
visitEd by alGaE
and maGical sEa-bEiNGs,
chERished by staRfish aNd uRchiNs,
admiREd by thE gods of natuRE
aNd passiNG doiliEs,
aNd kissEd by small colouRful poutiNG
fish

Poem 3
was an
experiment.
It started off with thoughts about Margaret Mead,
a cultural anthropologist
who is credited for saying:

> *'Never doubt that a small group of thoughtful, commit-
> ted citizens can change the world; indeed, it's the only
> thing that ever has.'*

and a tune
which lingers with me
from a recording made
by an unknown old man
which has been made into a loop
with a philharmonic orchestra adding vibrancy

behind the old man's withering voice.
Awkward… can't remember the name.
I hummed it to Siri.
She didn't know

The sentences are glimpses
of small moments
using senses
that develop
into larger happenings
as I play with the narrative,
making new shapes
and starts
and ends
of sentences

The movement of hope
and change
through time
which can start
diminishingly
small

I wanted to capture hope
and possibilities
I also wanted to experiment with the word
GREEN
as
just
a
bunch
of
letters
spread through

the verses
changing the shape of words
and
reuniting
for the last verse

Changing Green (adagio)

Chorus (singing)

It would only have to be small
It would only have to be small
It would only have to be small

a tiny root system clinging
to the shallow crevice between rocks,
a few leaves forming,
pulling in the goodness
the sun freely dispenses,
knowingly watching the movement,
ready to play against
the upwards pull of the sun.
Where do the roots start and end?
they resemble the creeping line of the gap
they follow,
hollowing out the space,
searching,
nimble,
as flexible
as a free form movement
of the letter 'G'
drawn

It would only have to be small
It would only have to be small
It would only have to be small

the flicker at the corner of her lips
as she brushes
the uneven bits
of her newly cropped fringe
away from her eyes,
remembering the sound
of the scissors
as they began
the transformation
she has been yearning for,
watching her parting hair
fall to the ground
in little chunks of childhood days
where choices
were never her own
the lettuce green dress
is left at home,
lying on her bed,
flouncing against the breeze,
tiny matching pointy shoes
on the floor
underneath

It would only have to be small
It would only have to be small
It would only have to be small

vibrations in the earth,
or the flutter of butterfly wings,
ground movements

that grow in volume,
friends who link arms,
trees silently connecting
below the surface,
unnoticed,
unheard,
unmentioned,
a green tree frog's
croak

It would only have to be small
It would only have to be small
It would only have to be small

the size of a fly's goggled eye
glowing green,
paused on a sticky leaf
covered with translucent aphids
sucking
the plant's sap flowing
from tree to aphid
in a single straw like
suck,
the green blood
of the tree
taken into the cone-shaped
mouth of the aphid,
the parasite,
the life
taker

It would only have to be small
It would only have to be small
It would only have to be small

an embryo making
the tiniest signs
of rocking
as it shares
movement
back and forth,
back and forth
back and forth
tempo
a pen follows the lines,
a sideways c,
a rocking chair,
half-moons
and a Christmas tree,
who would have
thought?

It would only have to be small
It would only have to be small
It would only have to be small

green written in a margin
of a grass stained,
grubby well-read book,
hurled out to sea
like pebbles with their shiny surfaces,
crashing together over millennia
green finds its way,
visited by algae
and magical sea-beings,
cherished by starfish and urchins,
admired by the gods of nature
and passing doilies,

and kissed by small colourful pouting
fish

It would only have to be small
It would only have to be small
It would only have to be small

the farewells and the endings

Regular pruning
by Dante DeBono

Sometimes in life we're met with troubles,
find ourselves tangled in the prickly brambles that come
up to meet us.
No velvety petals nor perfumed attar
make up for the thorns that catch on the fine skin of fingertips.
Roses stained with drops of blood aren't worth keeping.
Life asks you to prune it,
cut back damaged and diseased branches
to encourage new growth.
Holding on to decaying waste will only kill the rest of the plant.

he tells me about a blue house
in Elizabeth
where they smoked dope to pass the time
and he handed an envelope of money
to a man he didn't know
for a motorbike he didn't need

living on rolled oats and beer
while she survived on cigarettes, bad red wine
and all the photos of that time
look too perfect to be real
they're that yellow colour photos go
sound of the Triffids and the rotary phone
'speaking?'
light ever leaking and the poem repeating

it grew like a light, their love,
and then faded
arced over the city, the flightpath
of a fallen angel
or an injured bird
come home again
to be earthly and grateful
painful, living:
human

(J & S)
by Lily Roberts

cemetery, hot and grey
open sky a flat church roof for the pews of stones and markers
plinths for angels and obelisks reach
upwards like questing castle turrets
stripped of their lively banners
underneath, bones crowding out souls
and dead matter beautiful
kissing earth and timing decay, no
fire in the search for heaven left

the restful dirt makes me think
I'm happy
to cling to what I have
winged statue calls me sacred only as long
as she can't fly away
and I hear cars pounding the road nearby
questing after each other's taillights
the rich scent of blood and money
rolls off the city in waves

they wait at intersections
for their lives to change
on their way
here

(West Terrace)
by Lily Roberts

Invasive Species
by Chloe Cannell

Bang. The projectile bounced off my forehead and landed on the grass I was just eating. There was a chemical smell that burned my nose. The other animals around had fled the scene upon the loud noise. I raised my neck high to look for the source of the projectile. There was a being, not one I'd ever seen before, with little fair hair atop its head and blue eyes duller than the ones that looked back at me in a pool of water. It stood on two legs, not four like me and most of the other animals. It had stockier legs too than the birds that sometimes flew down to the ground to graze at seeds. The being stood in a ready position, like the larger animals—no larger than me—before they pounced on small ones. They never dared charge at me like this being did with the thing it held. I smelt the same chemical smell. The smoke blew lightly from the end of its tool. The being seemed surprised at what it had done.

Bang. I felt another projectile skim past me. I launched towards the being in full sprint. I needed the run. I needed the challenge. I needed the kill. It wouldn't threaten me or the other animals.

The being made noises. It seemed sad, like when the birds can't fly back up again. I didn't slow my charge. I would pummel the being until it was so soft it could only manage a whimper.

Roar. My mouth reverberated with my call. The ground shook under my hooves and I heard the projectile coming through the being's tool again, but this time throughout my whole body. It came through me. The projectile came through me. My mouth seared through the back and out my neck. It was burning through my mouth, and neck, and then the pain was throughout my head, and then the rest of my body was burning, and I was falling, and I was burning, and I was falling. I was on the ground. I wanted to raise myself up but now I was the desperate bird, dying in the dirt. My eyes opened and closed as the burning continued. The being was beside me with its weapon of killing. The death bringer.

The being's forepaw touched my forehead and gently stroked me. It whispered noises. All noises were softer. I'd never heard sound so quiet apart from sleep.

The death bringer had killed me. Our way of life disrupted.

I felt light.

Reaper
by Aden Burg

On one of the three dilapidated red fabric seats within the grungy, outdated laundromat sat a grim reaper. Her long white hair stretched past her shoulders, contrasting against the black flower pattern on her crimson kimono. The gaze of her pantone eyes was focused upon two groups of people: a middle-aged couple on the far machine, and a group of kids on the nearest machine. The couple's load was still occupied and it seemed as though it would be occupied for quite some time more. The wife tapped her foot back and forth. She sighed between glares at the digital timer that flashed dull green numbers. Erstwhile, her pudgy husband in the business suit scratched his unkempt head as he awkwardly stared at the surprisingly thriving green plants that rested to the far left of the reaper's seat. The reaper found the scene fascinating, humans never ceased to surprise her.

At the same time, she also observed the four kids who energetically pulled clothes from the machine closest to her. The eldest was a blond sixteen-year-old boy, who wore an emerald green t-shirt and lacquer denim jeans. It seemed he was overseeing the three much younger children and making sure they were not too rowdy. The reaper managed to observe both scenes since she could easily see both from her seat. She carefully stared at both in silence. She remained as such until the blond boy looked directly at the reaper. He waved at her, to which she could not help but blink. With a chuckle, the boy strode and seated himself next to her.

'Hey there, pretty lady. What kind of spirit are you?' he asked calmly.

'I am a grim reaper. I look after the souls of the departed,' she answered with a small smile.

'Oh, I see.'

'Are you a spirit medium?'

'Yeah, more or less. I mean, apparently our family used to be Shamans centuries ago. So maybe I alone inherited that power,' the boy shrugged.

'You alone... How lonely...' The reaper put her kimono sleeve to her face. Her eyes became downcast.

'Nah, it's not bad at all. I mean, my parents believed and supported me all the way. Besides, because I have this power, I'm able to reassure my siblings that the ghosts and boogiemen they imagine are not under their beds,' the boy chuckled.

'So it is a power which binds you to others... How rare and fascinating.' The reaper gazed into the boy's deep blue eyes.

'You're pretty rare and fascinating yourself, miss reaper. You're the first of all the spirits I've met who's a reaper. Plus, you're cute, kind, and a conversationalist. Not at all what anyone would think of a reaper.' The boy beamed into the reaper's crimson eyes.

'I see... That is... Not unpleasant to know.' The reaper nodded. A distinct tinge of red fell upon her cheeks.

'So, then, just what is an oddball grim reaper like you doing in a laundromat in the middle of the day?' the boy finally asked.

'I am... Curious about the living. Over the millennia of my existence I have always wondered how you all are simultaneously carefree in the presence of death, yet also shadowed by it in equal measure,' she continued passionately.

'Huh, I never thought about that... I guess... Thing is, life just keeps on going. That's all it is, like those plants up there.' The boy pointed to the pot plants. The reaper's gaze followed his finger.

'How so?'

'We feel sad and worried about how they'll die, that they won't last forever. But it's because of that, that these plants are pretty. I mean, those brief experiences and memories are what give us meaning and courage even when we're scared about dying. That's what it's like.' The boy smiled.

'I see... Hm... How interesting...' The reaper nodded as she stroked her chin.

'Glad you think so. My family's heading out now, so I gotta go. We're back here all the time though, so if you want to chat, feel free to meet me here again.'

'Yes, I may do that.'

'Alright. I'll see you around.' The boy waved and rejoined his family. The reaper watched and smiled.

'So this is the beauty of life? Truly, what a masterpiece.'

Gold Dust
by Anneliese Abela

Your eyes were green, soft like the airy sage of seaside waves, and the olive hue of our pine tree atop the hill between your home and mine. They were a deeper forest pigment in the darkness, the two of us whispering by torchlight in my small-panelled bedroom or sprinting down the empty road at midnight, the only ones alive in our firefly world.

Days of laughter, of obnoxious jokes and far-fetched tales, lying on the neighbour's manicured buffalo lawn and writing a song with all the words that rhyme with 'wish'. Nights spent launching peanut M&Ms into the air, shrieking at each loud clink against our teeth. A scratched DVD of *Holes* replaying until sunrise. Our effortless recital of the film's entire script.

Everything was easy, childlike, and free. Until it wasn't. Until I tangled it up. I was good at it, at spinning without direction until everything was a mess of knots. But you never ripped the thread, refused to cut yourself loose. You took the time to unravel us, no matter the pain it caused you, and despite my failure to promise not to do it again.

A well-trekked path maps our daily uphill climb, the pair of us dragging our feet over uneven ground to the tree at the top which we've claimed as our own, a stolen golden bauble glinting on the highest pine needle branch. Our leather school shoes were covered in dust—burs and nettles stuck to navy woollen jumpers.

You teach me to dance on your smooth concrete driveway. Your legs shuffle back and forth to electronic music and your fluoro-yellow hoodie is pulled up over your sandy blond head. Your freshly pierced earlobe, still swollen and pink, wearing one lime green stud while I wear the other. A pack of coloured earrings purchased after school, twelve pairs split up so we each took six nickel studs home. Early morning text messages to agree on the next colour. My lime green stud still hides at the bottom of my jewellery box, the nickel busted and bent out of shape.

Countless low-resolution photos snapped on Motorola phones: you flip me the bird as I throw a peace sign, your school tie pulled up around your head and chapped lips pursed, my dark eyes creased at the corners and tongue poking out. Fleeting glances of something deeper, captured in grainy colour and black and white. Unnoticed at the time but clear as glass now.

Nothing was really as murky as it appeared, none of it as complicated as we made it out to be. But I had nothing but a clouded vision in my youth.

A kiss beneath our spindly pine tree, as the sun dips low beyond the hill. My phone buzzing in my pocket—my parents want me home. But I am safe, for I'm with you. I hold your hand as the light disappears from the sky, and allow your hopes to wander, letting them gather speed to a racing pace. Our entwined fingers are a silent promise I know I will one day break.

And when it does eventually happen, it shatters you like our glass bauble ripped away by a harsh winter storm, leaving jagged gold shards littered on the grassy hill, the pine tree left shaken, branches stripped bare by howling winds. But you stay, and push your own heartache aside each time I run to you, your hands tangling in my hair as I cry into your chest over other boys who would never love me as much as you.

Your voice in my ear as you reassure me over and over: *everything will sort itself out.*

The months roll on and we sweep up the pieces together, and use the crushed golden dust to fill the cracks formed between us.

Surviving buds sprout on pine tree stems, fresh new growth viridescent.

We grow, and search far and wide to see where our hopeful visions for the future take us. We drift apart as life pulls at the tide, but find our way back with every exhale of the ocean. Our childhoods forced to a grinding halt at the sudden death of our close friend, followed by the drawn-out death of my father. We fulfil the old echoed promise of losing touch with schoolmates, despite how fiercely we push against it.

I move away, the distance between us much farther to cross, the effort more strenuous than a dusty uphill climb. But the gravity of your orbit pulls me back when I lean in close enough, and we find ourselves once more snacking on peanut M&Ms, inventing ridiculous stories of jet-ski shark attacks, and laughing at *Holes* as if for the very first time. You drive me back to the hill, point out our steadfast tree amongst the dense undergrowth, scattered yellow-green saplings sprouting up where fallen pinecone seeds have stretched their roots.

Our tree taller, stronger, everlasting.

My twenty-first birthday, in a crowded pub where music thrums through the floorboards. Drinks spill, shoes sticking with each tipsy step, a haze of smoke drifting out across the dancefloor. We bump shoulders at the bar, eyes alight, faces bathed in a deep purple spotlight. I stumble into your chest, your hands in my hair. My ribs crushed as you lift me off the ground.

Blond hair as messy as ever, long pale limbs in a white t-shirt and dark jeans. The two of us sink into a low leather couch, armrest fabric ripped and peeling. Each stupid joke repeated, each old story reminisced. Tears at the corners of our eyes and stitches in our sides. An overflowing beer in your hand, a little gel in your hair. I clutch at your arms as your knees knock into mine.

You fall silent. A shift of the light in your bloodshot eyes. Your voice cracks, mouth moving faster than I can keep up with, the words spilling from you, desperate and frantic.

My intoxicated mind can't grasp too tightly to anything. I reach for your hand, and feel your pulse race and fingers tremble. And then you stop, almost as quickly as you started, your slurred words of despair enduring like the haunting afterglow of lightning splashed across the skies.

I'm sorry, you say. *I shouldn't be telling you all this. It's fine—never mind.*

And before I can do so much as open my mouth, the smile is plastered back onto your face, a joke once more at the edge of your throat.

And I let you tell it.

The phone call wakes me. It takes a while to see through the heavy fog of my hangover, the hazy disbelief that casts an eerie mirage before my eyes, half-convincing me that they're wrong, that you're still here. My phone screen cracks as it hits the tiles, pain pulsing through my bones as my knees drop to the floor. A jolt to my heart as it hits me, each cracked syllable you uttered bouncing off my skull.

I work up the courage to drive past the hill, a shining golden bauble perched safely in tissue paper, price tag still tied to its string.

But our tree is gone, the land cleared for development, our well-trodden path erased and every forest green pine needle carted off in a skip—the olive hue of your eyes to be found only in grainy, low-resolution photographs.

And your words play over and over again in my head. *Everything will sort itself out.*

I recite them and ask myself why I never spoke them aloud, wonder whether hearing them might have been enough to make you stay.

What if I Called You Wally?
by Simon-Peter Telford

Last night's rain drizzled down off the corrugated iron sheet roof of a small and lonesome cottage. Atop a seaside cliff, the cottage sat, falling into its isolation and age. A major storm had wreaked havoc across the coastline as lightning and wind performed their pantomime in the cloudy theatre. Vincent had fought off the weariness of his old age the night before and was a captivated audience for the maelstrom. He continued to watch long after he would usually be slumped asleep in his cushioned chair next to his small potbelly fire. Filled with trinkets of the past, his home usually held his attention with an open book or a collection of photos from his youth, yet they could not compete with the slashing rain and rolling thunder. Eventually, sleep came for Vincent and took him after he shuffled into his wooden bed with its feathered pillows and thick, warm quilts.

The rain that drummed him to sleep returned to wake him this morning with a percussion of steady drops trickling off the gutter. Vincent rubbed at his watery blue eyes. He lifted his short legs out from under the layers of covering, with the ginger movement that came with the privilege of getting old. Vin patted the uppermost layer with a smile on his face. She had made this many years ago. It was all he had left of their marriage. Soon the kettle was screaming to life in preparation for his ritualised morning tea accompanied by two slices of bread that were well on their way to becoming toast.

After breakfast, Vincent decided on a shower to help him wake a little more. The copper pipes groaned like his body as the hot water rushed through them and down over his spotted head. Warm and refreshing, the water ran over him. Droplets trickled through the white hair that was left on his head. He felt the water trace the lines of his once muscular and stocky frame. The comforting warmth streamed down his thin legs, vanishing deep into the drain of his cream-coloured tub with its polished brass fixtures and handles.

Vincent hummed a tune before allowing the words to come tumbling out of his mouth. It was an old song that had carried him through the war, through his life. The towel came to his hand naturally as he stepped out to dry himself off. Vincent laughed. *Where has the man of my youth gone?* he thought to himself. He stood before the mirror, trying to see any hint of his former face behind the enveloping skin and deep wrinkles that now cloaked it. The eyes, he decided. It was the eyes that still held something of the days gone by where he didn't feel just so ancient in the mornings. True, those once pools of crystal blue may be blearier and more sunken than they were fifty years ago. They were not the same eyes. Yet, if he peered into his reflection, he could see the glint he had shown as a young lad.

Changing into a pair of pants and a blue polo top he slipped into his favourite walking shoes. A short time later Vin pushed open the front door of his cottage. He stepped into the rising sunlight as the last drops of rain splashed upon his head. The coastal cottage was adorned with a cheerful red-painted door and green corrugated iron for a roof. This was his small piece of the world. He had never been more happy, sad, lonely, and comfortable anywhere else in the world. After taking in a deep breath, allowing the salty air to fill his lungs, Vin let out a yawn and surveyed the damage of last night's storm. His property seemed mostly unscathed except for the shade cloth, now strewn amongst the branches of a nearby Banksia. The little tool shed was the largest casualty. It had stood for a decade before collapsing under the weight of the rain and the pounding of sea winds. Vincent's chocolate brown Leyland was parked under the carport. He loved that car, with its orange pinstripes down the side. The Leyland had stopped running only some days earlier when Vincent tried to start up the old girl. He wished it was working this morning. He would need to go into town and get some nails to repair the shed. After staring at the car with a scrunched-up face, he decided that a walk to the nearby beach would do for now.

Vincent started his journey with the cold wind beating against his exposed arms and face. He did his best to keep his back straight and his steps measured. An old habit he had been taught a lifetime ago. Gravel crunched under the soles of his shoes as Vin strolled down the little path leading from his front door, past the now ruined vegetable beds, and along the winding driveway that ended a hundred metres or so at the edge of his property. He pushed the waist-high gate open, with a jingle from a rusted bell attached to the frame and headed down the road. Vincent's feet banged out the beat of a march within his head while he began to whistle an old Merchant's tune.

The sun worked to warm his somnolent muscles and with each step he could feel his strength return to him. Several minutes later he strolled past a dilapidated windmill. Standing solitary in its field of swishing long grass he strode past without taking a second glance. Vin's knees started to burn as the downward slope of the bitumen road began to increase.

Another half-hour and Vincent had passed all the landmarks he would usually drive by when the temperamental Leyland decided to cooperate: a giant silver water tank that served for irrigation to some long-gone farmer, the hill covered in bushes of Silver Daisy that stood out like a giant pile of sugar against the coastal scrubland, and finally the tiny car park that was nestled at the top of the beach before a small beaten path down onto the sand. Vin's legs shook slightly when he came to a halt and he rested against one of the wooden pylons that surrounded the parking area. His head felt like there was a hand of stone grasping him.

'Whew,' Vincent breathed out and let the air whistle between his pink lips. *It's been a while since I've made that walk*, he thought.

He trudged on through the car park until he arrived near the sand where, stooping low, he worked the laces on his trainers. Vincent lowered himself down onto the soft grass that sprouted from a miniature oasis between the dead and lifeless bitumen and the coarse unforgiving sand. He slid his shoes and white sports socks off his worn feet that had carried him these past seventy-eight years. He wiggled his toes in the grass, feeling the freshness and life. The socks he rolled up into a ball and tucked away inside one of his shoes before, eventually, pushing himself to his feet with a groan.

He took a few steps forward and felt his feet sink into the cool sand. Onward he walked, following a thin path through the maze of spindled flora that dotted the golden dunes. Eventually, he came to the crest of one such dune and peered down at the small beach that was his alone to enjoy. The white sand stretched out to the reddish-brown cliffs which ran along the edge to the east, where his cottage stood far above. Waves were rolling in like the heartbeat of the ocean, crashing over themselves in a sparkling blue and white torrent of raging water before being spread out along the wet sand. Vincent smiled, taking it all in. He could see that some of the cliff face had collapsed during the dark of night and huge piles of stinking brown and green seaweed were regurgitated onto the beach during the havoc of the storm.

A black object caught his eye further down along the beach. Vin couldn't make out any distinctive features except that it must have been extraordinarily large. His stomach sank as realisation began to dawn. His bare feet sprayed sand in all directions as he ran towards the long, sleek object. The deep sand slowed his progress and tore at his calves until he reached the wet foreshore. The waves desperately stretched out onto the beach before receding into their world of water. The hurried rush of his feet dominated the empty beach. The slapping noise added a steady beat to the sound of crashing waves.

Vincent was close now and dread had crept inside his mouth. 'Oh no. Oh dear, no,' he exhaustedly muttered as he came up next to the beached whale. It was larger than any living thing Vin had seen. The whale was stranded on its stomach and had been for some time. The water behemoth was old from what he could tell. Many barnacles had formed along its thick skin. Vin's mind worked hard for some sort of solution.

The whale was about fifteen metres from the water's edge and must have been beached in the ravenous storm during the night. After several frantic minutes circling the whale, which included giving an experimental but hopeless tug of its massive tail back towards the sea, Vincent gathered himself and walked his way towards the head. Once he found the creature's eye, tiny in comparison to the rest of its body, he levelled himself with it. The eye was surrounded by creases in the skin. It was a rich blue like the habitat it came from and still sparkled with life. Vin stared at the eye for a long time. He came to recognise terror and death swirling in the blue.

'Hello,' Vin said, placing a hand on the grey skin. The skin looked and felt like a rubber prune. 'It's okay,' he soothed, knowing that the whale could not understand him but not knowing what else he could do. 'I'm not going to hurt you. I've just got to figure out how to help.' Gently rubbing his hand back and forth, Vincent did his best to relax the poor mammal. Taking a few steps back to hopefully identify its species he inspected the whale from top to tail. It was about sixteen metres long and its skin was a deep grey with some white markings creeping up from the underbelly. It was taller than Vincent too, almost seven and a half feet. When he trudged his way to its mouth a row of large white teeth poked out from its gums. Vin thought hard, scouring deep inside his brain for any whale knowledge that he may have tucked away with his information on local fishes and other obscure pieces of understanding one picks up from living next to the ocean.

A whale with teeth, he thought to himself as he rubbed his chin. Now, what whale has teeth and is a local. About fifteen metres long and grey with small eyes. 'A sperm whale!' he blurted out as the answer came to him. 'You're a sperm whale, aren't you, sir?' Rubbing its skin again with his tanned hands he whispered, 'I'm going to get help, alright? But I'm going to have to go back home and use my telephone. I'll be back as fast as I can, I promise.' The whale seemed to look straight into his eyes when he spoke. Vincent found pulling his hand off the shrivelled skin and turning his back on it wrenched his heart.

His legs hurt, his bones hurt, and his breathing still hadn't fully recovered but Vin took off running back the way he had just came with newfound adrenaline pumping through his veins. Before long he was back to the dunes and crashing through the shrubbery that left his pants ripped around the cuffs. He pushed his body past the empty car park and continued up the sloping hills that lead to his little cottage. The dying whale he had left behind urged his every step and it wasn't until after he had sped past the daisy-covered hill and the silver water tank that Vincent realised he hadn't stopped to put his shoes back on at the car park. His feet were raw and bleeding from the coarse road and his head felt fit to burst.

He crashed through the door of his cottage and hastily pushed past stacks of paper until he found his telephone. It was old, brass coloured and corded with the old-fashioned circular dial on the front. Vincent's hand shook as he grabbed at it and dialled the number for emergency services. Pressing the phone to his ear he was met with a crushing silence. There was nothing, no dial tone, no interference of any kind, nothing except damning silence that screamed louder than any response ever could.

'Damn,' Vin cried as he threw the useless machine to the ground in anger. He shuffled outside and found a tree branch that had torn down the thin telephone line running to his house from the street. 'Damn,' he repeated and, turning on his heels, Vin rushed back inside for the keys to his Leyland. He plucked the jangling metal from an overturned seashell that was used as a bowl and sprinted back through to the car. Throwing the Leyland's driver side door open he collapsed onto the seat and thrust the keys into the ignition. Vincent turned the key hard and pumped his foot on the accelerator, willing the machine to work. The engine screeched in protest and spluttered. 'Work, you bloody thing! Work!' Vin pleaded as he smacked his fist on the steering wheel over and over again. The engine showed signs of life as it whirred and thrummed. Vincent thought he had won the battle.

But with one more clawing noise the old Leyland died in a smoky haze. Vincent lowered his head in defeat and exhaled. He felt a spell of dizziness come over him. He felt nauseous and sweat dotted his forehead. His old hands were shaking on the steering wheel as the exertion of today's events caught up with the seventy-eight-year-old. Vin's vision filled with black, and the steering wheel rushed up to meet him.

A short time later Vin's head slowly moved upright, and consciousness worked itself back through his body. He rubbed at his forehead that sported a slight bruise from crashing down onto the wheel. Taking a few deep breaths Vincent opened the door and stood on shaky legs using the Leyland for support. *I won't make it through another marathon like that*, he thought. He gradually made his way back inside and went to the sink where he splashed water over his face and neck before drinking a glass. As he sipped at the refreshing liquid an idea blossomed in his head. Vin quickly gathered a few biscuits and stuck them inside his pocket. The small shed that sat behind his house held a slightly rusted bicycle and Vin decided that it would be in enough of a working order to get him back down to the beach.

After several minutes of wrestling with the handlebars, he coached the bike out from its position among shovels and paint cans. Vincent hopped on the bike with newfound resolve and pedalled his way down the driveway once again towards the beach. Riding his bicycle was a much better option than walking, with the ground's natural decline making for easy travel. The windmill, shed, daisy hill, and car park all flew by him in no time at all. After stopping to eat a biscuit, as a precaution, Vin headed back out along the sand towards the sad sight. Approaching the great sperm whale, he laid a hand in the same spot he had around an hour ago. Slowly rubbing the dry thick skin, Vin let his head hang in disappointment.

'I'm sorry, friend,' he said, his voice croaking. 'I don't think I'll be able to help you... I can't save you.' He slumped down onto the soft sand next to the stranded giant and heard it make a low groaning sound. Vincent stared out across the rolling waves and found that for the first time in a very long time he didn't know what to do. *I suppose all I can do is keep the old boy company. No one should have to die alone.*

The two of them sat next to each other in silence for quite some time before Vin suddenly turned back to the whale's miserable eye and spouted, 'You got a name?' He wasn't quite sure how to continue, it was a very strange feeling. It was an odd thing to be sitting next to a creature that seemed larger than life and yet was dying. He knew that whales had some sort of intelligence as far as creatures went, and he knew that they were also quite social, but Vin had no way to communicate with the poor animal. He had talked to dogs and said hello to the odd cat like most people find themselves doing from time to time but this helpless whale seemed on another level.

'What if I called you Wally?' Vincent asked in a way that suggested he cared about the whale's thoughts on its new name. 'Wally the whale,' he continued. 'That sounds pretty good, doesn't it? I knew a Wally once, but that was back when I was a lad in England.' He stopped and moved a little closer to the goliath, determined to at least keep a conversation going, even if it was rather one-sided. 'He was a childhood friend in a little village, part of the Swaton county of Lincolnshire. It was a small village, but it had a wonderful old church with great big stained-glass windows and was simply a magical place to live as a child.' Vin kicked at some of the sand closest to his feet and felt a small piece of wood dig into the side of his big toe. Rubbing at it he continued, 'My father was a sexton there and he would have to be up at four in the morning on Sundays to make sure the stoves were all lit in the church. It was so dreadfully cold in England, see.' He gave Wally's side a light slap for emphasis and said not unkindly, 'I bet a great fat thing like yourself would be fine with the cold though. Lots of blubber to keep you warm.' He laughed at this, but the laughter trailed off. 'I had three older brothers, but they all died very young from diphtheria,' Vin said in a flat voice. 'I had a sister too, but she died as well. Fork straight to the temple. At the dinner table, poor thing. It was an accident of course but I don't think my cousin ever really did get over that.'

Wally let loose a few deep clicking noises and tried to breathe through his blowhole. Vin took off his shirt and waded into the water about knee-deep before plunging the fabric underneath, using it as a makeshift bucket. He then quickly waddled back over with the captured sea sloshing over the sides of his polo shirt. He dumped the shirt over a portion of the whale's side, near its head but Vin knew it had little to no effect. He could do this all day without making the slightest bit of difference to Wally's suffering, so instead he sat back down with his back up against the whale's side and gave the giant another pat. 'Yes, England was much different to here. I don't even know if they get sperm whales up that far.'

Vin took another biscuit from his pocket and nibbled on it, speaking between mouthfuls. 'We had a reasonably big house. Four bedrooms with lots and lots of vegetables in the garden and pigs and hens and chickens all over the place. The butcher would come round, and I would hate it,' he explained as crumbs flew from his mouth. 'The pigs would squeal so terribly when they were slaughtered. Once I grew to be very fond of one pig in particular. I called him Percy. He had the curliest tail you'd ever seen on a pig, not that I suppose you have ever seen one. Anyway, one day I came home from school to find out that my dad had sold the pig to some neighbours of ours and that the butcher had come to slaughter it.' Vin crunched down the last of the biscuit and said, 'I don't think I ate pork again for the next year at least. Dad was also a headmaster at the local school, so I don't think he ever cared for his son spending all hours of the day and night playing with Percy the pig, rather than studying.'

The whale let out another collection of clicks and groans. They were low, strained. It was the sound of water gurgling in a sink. Vincent's heart broke at the sounds as he tried to softly soothe Wally. He went and fetched another shirt full of water to dump over the whale's back this time. 'Do you have a girlfriend, Wally? Or perhaps a wife or mistress? I remember seeing a girl when I was still quite young. Her name was Pauline, but we all called her Polly. Sounds a bit like your name, doesn't it? Well, Polly was very attached to me but unfortunately, I just didn't have the same feelings. It was fun to kiss a girl being a young boy and inexperienced, but once you had done it a couple of times it kind of loses its magnetism, don't you think? I can still hear my father yelling at me for breaking things off with her. I had walked home after giving her my farewell when my father began telling me how ungrateful I was to Polly. As it turns out, she had been round just a few hours earlier and given Father three rabbits for dinner. I don't think I had ever tasted anything more full of shame in my life than the rabbit stew we had that night.'

Vincent had found talking to Wally easier than he thought it would be. Maybe it was the isolation he had been living in or maybe it was pity or perhaps the uncomfortable feeling of watching a fellow living thing die. Either way, Vin was soon jabbering on about his school years, his best friend Jack, the charm of Swaton, and the memories of a childhood he held dear. Wally would, on occasion, make a low grunting noise or wheeze from his blowhole but it was clear to Vin that the whale was rapidly declining.

Vin saw a plastic bottle being hurled through the foaming waves and watched as it wrestled with the currents before eventually being spat onto the beach. His brow crinkled in anger at the sight of the litter, so he slowly rose to his feet to collect it. Once down on the wet, hard-packed sand he stretched down for the bottle, feeling a slight pain in his chest as he did.

When Vincent stood back upright he saw with horror that a large sea eagle had landed on top of Wally's helpless body and had begun to claw at his flesh with sharp talons and a razor beak. Vin let out a yelp and quickly ran back over to Wally's side. He threw his arms in the air and shouted at the eagle. It pushed itself several metres into the air, beating its astonishing wings as it screeched at the interruption. Vin thought he had succeeded in scaring off the wicked thing, but it only circled back around and landed slightly further down Wally's back before going to work yet again.

'Get off, you great bloody bastard,' Vincent roared at the eagle as he tried to swipe at it, but as much as he tried Vin could not reach up past Wally's enormous side. He turned and scanned the beach before seeing a long black piece of driftwood thirty metres or so up the coast. Vin ran for it. He could feel the tightening in his chest again, but he chose to ignore it as he dived into the sand with outstretched hands. He felt his old fingers curl around the salted wood, and like a broadsword, he held it out in front of himself with both hands at one end as he stalked back to Wally and his attacker.

'Clear off now or I'll have you,' Vincent bellowed. The Eagle either didn't hear him or plain didn't care.

'Right,' Vincent said. He jumped up and smacked the bird in the side of its folded wing. There was an immediate noise of surprise from the eagle and feathers flew as it took off into the air. Vin watched the white and grey bird of prey soar higher into the air before circling back around and heading straight for him. Vin steeled himself and tightened his grip on the driftwood in his hands. The eagle dived and picked up speed, its pointed beak flashing in the sunlight. Closer and closer it charged, splitting the air in an attack evolutionarily perfected as the distance between them was eaten up.

Vincent thought the eagle was going to smash right into him but milliseconds before they connected the white belly threw out its wings in a brilliant arc and lunged with its nasty talons. Vin managed to bring his driftwood up in time as the eagle's attack bowled him over in a shower of sand and seaweed. He had escaped being torn by its knife-like weapons. He spat coarse sand out of his mouth and tried to get the dry taste out as he watched the white-bellied sea eagle fly off into the distance. He tried to stand and felt the tightness in his chest, worse this time.

He staggered with heaving breaths back over to inspect Wally's wounds. They were deep but not deep enough to cut through all the layers of fat and protective blubber that encompassed the whale.

'You're alright, Wally mate,' he wheezed as he slowly slid down the side of the giant. They sat there in silence before Vin began to sing in a low murmured voice. He was still singing that same old merchant tune he loved so much. Vincent knew whales sung to each other and hoped that maybe Wally would get something out of it. Not the words or the meaning behind the lyrics but maybe the melody. He hoped his soft reassuring voice would be able to transcend the unimaginable gap between man and beast in some way. Wally, for his part, lay there, his eye no longer looking into Vin, but through him.

Vin stretched his legs out in front of him. They looked skinnier than usual, almost like the last of his strength and vigour had been sucked dry from today's gruelling pace. 'Bing Crosby sings it the best in my opinion. That man had a voice that could soothe even last night's storm.' He repeated the last word of the song in a low resounding note before continuing with his one-sided conversation. 'That was our song, my wife and I. She was the love of my life and I miss her more and more with each day that passes. My friend Jack introduced us. You remember Jack, right? Well, as I said earlier, Jack and I were childhood friends. I had joined the Merchant Navy when the war broke out and had worked my way up to boatswain.' Vin stopped as all the memories of the high seas came flooding back to him. 'Don't worry. I'll tell you all about that later. Lots of ocean. I'm sure you'll be very interested. Anyway, I was on leave and had lots of money to spend as young navy men did on leave. Jack's girlfriend, and later to be his wife, Elsa took Jack and myself to a dance being held on base at a nearby army compound. I decided I was tired of wasting half my wage on cheap booze for half of London, so I agreed.'

Vincent's eyes had started to shine with the memories he was sharing, and he hadn't stopped smiling since mentioning his wife. He hadn't smiled like this in quite some time. Making random spirals and shapes in the sand with his finger he continued, 'Her name was Joan. She was a private in the anti-aircraft division and worked to plot German bombers coming over England. From what she told me she would then pass the data on to the gunners. I had my crisp whites on as any reputable merchantman would and I can still remember Elsa and Joan huddling like two schoolgirls by the bar as Joan weighed me up. She was so beautiful, and I could tell that she was spoilt for choice when it came to men. But I must have been looking pretty damn good that night because later Elsa told me that Joan had said she liked the look of me. We danced all night long together.' Vincent looked fit to burst with happiness. 'Swirling and dipping on the dance floor. I tell you, Wally. It is truly a magical thing. Looking into a woman's eyes, everything else melts away,' he said. 'The terrible war, the death, and destruction all around us. London was in pieces but all of that just disappeared when I looked into her eyes and felt her hand in mine.'

Vincent felt a drop of water run down his face and his first thought was that it must have started raining. It was not rain but rather tears dripping down his creased, tan skin. He quickly wiped at them with the back of his hand before clearing his throat. 'After Jack and I left that dance I told him I was going to marry that woman, and I did. I didn't know she was already engaged at the time though,' he revealed, laughing slightly as he did. 'War, Wally. It does strange things to people. I nearly died in the sea myself. Not very far out, mind you. I was in a harbour.'

Wally made another one of his croaking noises and Vin hurried to fill his shirt with water again. After giving the whale a few consolidating pats and doing his best to clean the sand from Wally's eye Vincent went on, 'We had come in for the usual repairs and to restock supplies. It was the middle of the night when the bomb hit, and I tell you now, I have never heard such a noise in all my life. I was only twenty-two and I thought I was going to die that night. Water was pouring in, and we were sinking fast, not to mention the fires and live electricity all over the place. I lost a few friends in the madness that followed but almost everyone managed to abandon ship and swim to the harbor.' Vin rubbed his chin as he spoke. His voice had lowered and his eyes narrowed as he stared out into the ocean. The sun was starting its descent and judging by its position in the sky it must have been late afternoon already. These memories still haunted him, even now.

'We were married during the war, Joan and I,' Vincent said after a long time. 'In Swaton, my home village, at the old church. It was still wartime, so things were a little tight. Joan's auntie was a beauty queen and gave her beauty gown to Joan to wear and, by God, Wally. She was the most beautiful woman I had ever laid eyes on. All my aunties rationed food together and put on a tremendous feast. My father even killed a pig so there was plenty of ham to go around.'

Vin stood and strolled up and down next to Wally. His back hurt and moving helped. He let all aspects of the whale sink in. He touched its massive pectoral fin gently and ran his fingers between the creases that spun like spider webs. He continued to talk as he made his way around to the other side of Wally for, what he realised, was the first time since meeting him.

'We didn't see each other on the day until we were at Church, but I can still remember her mother saying to me, "Today you are taking my daughter from me, and if you don't treat her right, I'll be taking her back".' He laughed fondly at the memory but then stopped.

On Wally's right side there was a wide gash just above his underbelly. The bloody wound was almost four feet long and about a foot wide. It oozed dark blood and the stench coming from it was foul.

'Oh, Wally, what have you done?' Vincent asked as he raised his hand to cover his mouth. He placed a shaking finger onto the wound and felt something sharp sticking out through it. Vin gently prodded at a slick metal rod that was protruding like a bloody flag on a grey moon. Wally tried to shift his weight against the pain Vin knew must be wracking his body. The mammal shifted on the coarse sand and managed to move a few pathetic inches.

'Sorry about that,' Vin said, positioning himself to get a better view of the gash, though he knew it would be impossible to see how much metal could be buried beneath the whale's flesh. Hope had all but dried up for Wally. Even if Vin could somehow get the whale back in the churning water, he was unlikely to survive. There was only one thing left to do. He would sit by Wally and keep him company. Vincent was overcome with a sadness that made his eyelids tingle with the threat of tears. He had hidden a tiny sliver of hope that the sperm whale might make it out alive.

Vincent walked back around Wally to the groove he had fashioned from sitting next to the whale and lowered himself down. He gave Wally another heartfelt rub just above the eye and watched the clouds, once heavy and grey, now white streaks across an endless blue sky. The smoothness of the unexpected late afternoon weather coupled with the smell of saltwater and the sound of waves reminded Vincent of his migration to Australia with his wife decades ago. He decided that he would keep talking to Wally. He had no idea if it was comforting to the big whale or not, but it was the best he could do.

'Joan and I crossed half the world or more to come here to Australia. You've probably done your fair share of travelling too, I assume.' He nodded towards the fading eye of Wally 'We had to get up at four o'clock in the damn morning for that trip. Lucky I got up at all, really. Joan and I travelled to London to catch a ship and her father was a blubbering mess when we left. I hope he eventually forgave me for taking his daughter so far from him.' A pained look flashed across Vin's face. 'And the number of bloody injections we had to have was ridiculous. I still have nightmares about those needles, as big as your arm, I swear it... Or your flipper I suppose.' Vin laughed, there was nothing else he could do. As his gaze fell back onto the repetitive crash and roll of waves lapping against the shore, he remembered how smooth the sea was on their voyage to Australia. 'The most comfortable trip ever if the captain was to be believed. You see, usually families were to be split up on the long voyage with men sleeping in separate rooms, but we were allowed to remain together which made the trip all that much better.'

'We saw a blue whale on our way over, absolutely magnificent,' Vin exclaimed as he rummaged around in his pockets for a particularly elusive biscuit. 'The size of that tail rising out of the water! I had never seen such a thing. Makes you look like a little snapper, Wally.' He found the biscuit and bit down on it. Vin wiped at some crumbs around his mouth. 'Jack and Elsa came over with us, thank God. I don't think I would have ever left if we didn't all go together. It was a great adventure that I'm still living to this day, and I am very glad to have met you along the way, Wally. I just wish it was under better circumstances.'

Several whales appeared out in the water. Vin could not believe it. The giants began to slap their wide dominating tails on the water's surface. Vin stood quickly to face the family of giants. The sudden rise made his head spin and daggers shot through his arm. He gathered his breath once more and waved out to the pod with his arms flailing in the air. He shouted greetings and danced around the place in the sand.

'Look, Wally! Is that your family?' he asked. He gave the whale several long strokes. Wally could not see the pod. He had washed up with his head facing toward land. Vin tried to move his massive head so that Wally could see the whales causing a commotion out at sea. He pushed and pushed against the side of Wally's head. Vin's feet were ankle-deep in sand from the pressure of his efforts, but Wally hadn't budged one bit. Vincent suddenly slipped and crashed into the ground next to Wally, face first. A spasm of pain wracked Vin's body and he realized he had come down on his arm awkwardly.

'I'm sorry. I can't—I can't move you, Wally. I'm sorry,' he said as he lay there on the sand next to the sixteen-metre long animal. Vin felt tired, more tired than he had in a long time. He raised his head and looked eye to eye with Wally. 'You can hear them, can't you, sir?' he asked, spitting out sand as he did. 'You may not be able to see them, but I know you can hear them. The whales have come to comfort you and they won't let you die alone.' He crawled back over to the side of the now almost unbearably pungent whale and put his back up against it. 'And neither will I,' he said. 'I left some of my best friends to die that night we were bombed. I will not do the same to you.' Vin massaged his aching arm and tried to collect his thoughts. They sat there together listening to the thunderous sound of the pod's affection. For an hour they slapped their tails and blew water high into the air through blowholes but eventually, as the sun began to descend more and more and the night started its silent invasion, the whales slowed down and stopped altogether.

Vin slipped his worn leather wallet out and rifled through cards before finding the photo he was after. The cards and his photo were wet and crumpled. He hadn't thought to empty his pockets when going into the water. The small photo had been by his side for decades. It most likely would not survive the night. Still, Vin held the small memory up to Wally's eye. 'See, there's Joan.' He pointed to a regal-looking woman with short curly hair and piercing eyes but who wore a warm and friendly smile. She was standing with a younger version of Vincent from days long past.

'Cancer took her from me in the end,' Vin said, his demeanour changing. 'I don't talk about this, Wally, but I've told you pretty much everything else. We were on a holiday back in the United Kingdom, nineteen-eighty-nine. I'm not likely to forget that year anytime soon,' Vin explained. 'She developed a nasty cough while we were over there and constantly complained about not feeling well. So naturally, we went to the doctors and after a few tests, well, they found it. It was cancer. Lung cancer.' Vin stopped at this and gave Wally a concerned look. His breathing had become ragged at this point. 'Cancer is the *fucking* devil if you ask me. We spent Christmas Day at the hospital and on Boxing Day she was released, so we came back to Australia, only to start chemo shortly after we returned. For the first nine months or so everything went rather well. The tumours had shrunk, and everything was looking rather promising. She was a tough old girl, army tough, and I never doubted that we would make it through the hardship.' He had been subconsciously digging at the sand with clawed fingers as he spoke and had only now realized as his nail was split by a buried twig. Vin quickly popped his finger into his mouth and sucked on it to subside the pain.

The pinks of the setting sky and the radiant ball of orange sun like an egg yolk dangling just above the horizon bathed the two in colour. Vin swallowed and pressed on with the memory. 'She woke up one morning and told me in a scared voice that all the walls were moving. After more tests and doctors hovering around like flies, they informed me that the cancer had spread to her liver. In her last two weeks she suffered malignant meningitis in her spine. I won't go too much into her suffering, but it was far more than she deserved. Friends we had here were called in as death seemed to loom closer and after suffering a seizure we were told she would not live much longer.' Vin bit at his nail and cast his eyes into the sand. 'I feel very bad for this, Wally, and I have never forgiven myself...' he paused. 'But I wished her to die. I couldn't bear to see her like that. It wasn't right. It wasn't fair,' he yelled as anger boiled out of him and a seagull took to startled flight down the shore.

'I slept on the floor next to her bed every night she was in hospital, and I had loved her for all my life. I couldn't stand to see her drift in and out of consciousness, wracked with pain and deteriorating in front of my eyes. A nurse made the decision that I couldn't bring myself to make. I thank her every day in my prayers that she had the strength to do what I could not. The doctors took me into a room and gave us the grim details. They wanted us to play some sort of sick waiting game, holding our breath until she took her last but the nurse convinced the doctor to administer an extra dose of morphine to end Joan's pain.' There was a long silence in which Vin wiped at his mouth and face. 'I can remember it like yesterday, Wally. Just before they pumped in the morphine, I grasped her hand and said it's time to go, and Joan opened her eyes for a split second and winked at me, before passing away.'

There were tears rolling down Vincent's sand splattered face and his chest heaved with sobs. Vin was suddenly appreciative of just how isolated the beach was, as he hadn't allowed himself to break down like this in a long time. The tears rushed out like waves as Vin buried his head in his hand before pulling himself together a few minutes later. It was almost dark now on the beach and Vin could make out the lone streetlight that pitifully tried to illuminate the car park at the end of the sand. He unexpectedly became aware that Wally's long, rattling breaths had stopped. The groans and clicks that punctuated the silence from time to time had gone silent as well and his flesh somehow seemed colder than it was before.

Vin scrambled on his hands and knees over to Wally's eye and almost broke into tears again when he looked into it and saw Wally's eye staring through him, out into the night's sky, lifeless. A few small droplets managed to escape through Vin's lids before he could rush a hand up to his eye and stop them. He took a few sniffs to halt his running nose and placed a hand on Wally's side. 'I'm sorry, friend,' he said with a croak. 'I'm sorry I couldn't save you and more so I'm so very sorry you had to spend your last moments listening to an old man cry.'

The stars shined overhead in all their brilliance. Vincent felt quite cold and alone standing next to Wally's body on the solitary beach with the Milky Way glittering above. He sat with Wally's body for some time as the night grew darker but when the wind picked up and rain began to spit down on them once more, he decided it was time to leave. As Vincent turned and started his long walk back down toward the car park, along the moonlit shore, he softly sung in a deep and broken voice. Reaching the car park, Vin tried to brush the rain from his eyes. The storm had picked up tremendously in the short time he had walked the beach. It looked as if tonight's storm would rival the previous in ferocity and power. Wind pulled at his clothing and battered his frail body while far off lightning out to sea flashed and cut its way through the cloudy sky. He knew it was going to be a long and hard journey home, but Vin didn't care all that much. He was still feeling sort of numb after the death of Wally, like he was floating inches above the ground as he walked through the sheets of thick rain.

Time slipped by as Vincent trudged up the inclined road. Nature's wild fury buffeted him about the place. The rusted bike had broken its chain. The sugar hill of Silver Daisies was holding its own against the oncoming storm, but several large patches of the flower had been flattened by the torrential rain. His progress was slow as Vin's body protested loudly at the abuse it had taken throughout the day and night. His arm still hurt and he felt like an icy finger was burrowing its way into the middle of his chest. After some time, he passed the large water tank which looked ready to topple over. The storm was rolling with all its might onto land now and he couldn't help but think of poor Wally, who if he had survived, may have been washed back to freedom with the coming tides.

Vin was now shivering greatly in the cold and wet. He felt his body give massive shudders, trying to generate warmth within his archaic muscles. It was becoming harder to walk in a straight line and he had started to trip over his feet every now and then. He would suddenly stop and check his surroundings as if he had suddenly forgotten where he was going.

'I won't forget you anytime soon, Wally,' he said, trying to keep his mind off the numbing sensation crawling up his feet. 'A big old whale. Hey, fancy that.' The windmill was within his view, sitting just after a turn in the road and it raised his hopes. It mustn't be long now until he was within the shelter of his little cottage. Making his way past the decrepit windmill, with its blades spinning at an unimaginable speed, Vin's breathing was shallow but his shivering had stopped. He was completely unconcerned for his well-being as his mind was still down at the beach with Wally, talking of days gone by.

By the time he reached the gravelled driveway of the small white cottage with its red door and green roof, Vin was stumbling and the lightning above was blinding him. His feet dragged along the gravel, leaving a wake of rain-submerged stones behind him. The Leyland was illuminated in a burst of white and the destroyed tool shed seemed to rock from side to side. Vincent knew he had to make it to the red door. The red door was warmth. The red door was shelter. The red door was home. Vin reached out his hand and clasped the cold metal doorknob as the full strength of the storm exploded overhead. He turned it and collapsed inside in a pile of sodden clothes and freezing bones.

With all the strength left in his body, he heaved himself back up on his shaking knees and used his armchair for support. Shuffling over to a box tucked away under his coffee table, Vincent pulled out a dusty vinyl record. It was Bing Crosby's Greatest Hits and after blowing dust off the back cover and the struggle of his frozen mind working out the track numbers, Vin placed the record on an elegant record player that looked almost as old as he did. The scratchy recording, full of joy and raw detail crackled to life and soon a crooning voice and whimsical melody were filling the cottage.

Vin went into his bedroom and crawled into his bed, his body giving out on him halfway through, nearly pulling back the covers. He cocooned himself within the thick layers of warmth and let his eyes close, his breathing still very ragged and uneven. As the words to his song lofted to his ears Vincent said quietly, 'Goodnight, Wally. Until we meet again.'

author biographies
and statements

Anneliese Abela

Author Bio

Anneliese Abela is a writer and PhD candidate at the University of South Australia. Her creative pieces and news articles have been published both in print and online, and her research focuses on WWI history, Australian war literature, and the power of fiction in recapturing the past. She has recently finished her first historical novel: a tale of friendship, grief, and survival amidst the futility of war. Her writing can be followed on Instagram at @anneliese.abela.author

Author Statement

Green is memory: the smell of freshly-blended juice, the feel of prickly pine needles in your shoes, the sound of waves crashing to shore, the sight of green eyes in faded photographs. 'Desiderium' and 'Gold Dust' are memoirs, and explore how even the smallest memories bring someone we've once lost rushing back to us. The writing process for both pieces was led by emotion—sometimes joy, sometimes grief, sometimes regret—and was influenced by the power our senses hold in capturing and preserving memories.

The experience of 'green' in 'Desiderium' is found in my father's outlook on life and cancer. He believed in holistic healing and joined body, soul and nature together to extend his lifespan. As a young man he found a home in the ocean. Upon his death he returned there once more. 'Gold Dust' evokes the innocence and safety of childhood friendship and its natural evolution into something deeper, like a pine tree growing taller and stretching its roots deep underground.

It explores the fragility of life, shattered in an instant like a falling glass bauble, and how sometimes we can do nothing but sweep up the dusty fragments and try to move on, knowing nothing will ever be the same.

'Sentient Beings' takes place within a microcosm returned to a natural state, where animals are free to simply exist, unburdened by human interference. The natural world shapes the animals' lives, and the piece explores the journey from birth to death and this endless cycle's renewal. It intentionally omits human presence, action or thought, acknowledging the animals themselves as the protagonists of the piece to shine a light on the universal emotions experienced by all living beings.

Aden Burg

Author Bio

Aden Burg is an Adelaide-based creative writer who graduated from the University of South Australia with a Bachelor of Arts in English and Creative Writing. His detective short story, 'No Return', was published in the 2018 edition of the University of South Australia's creative writing anthology series *Piping Shrike*. Aden's passion is reading and writing fast-paced stories with unusual characters, a proclivity that bleeds into his research specialty of creative writing and visual storytelling in manga.

Author Statement

'Fresh Inspiration' is intended to convey how it feels to play a game of shogi with a friend. In that, this story conveys the strategic attribute of the game, the mindset that players have, and the literal feel of the playing the game. The story is dedicated to the visual, tactile, and taste sensations that occur around the protagonist. The most prevalent of these is tea, which is the drink that both players sip during play. However, players that do this are mostly those playing for fun or those who are playing with a friend. As such, the story was also used to convey the friendship between both players and how that drips into the game itself. The resulting piece reflects the mindset, physical sensations and connections behind a game of shogi.

'Reaper' is intended to convey how it is often the perceived boring attributes of life that are the most interesting. To illustrate this, 'Reaper' uses a gentle, female Japanese-styled reaper as an inhumane presence that is able to question and observe what most people cannot. Her presence and perspective are placed in this story so that readers can observe the unusualness and perhaps reconsider what they think is monotonous.

Chloe Cannell

Author bio

Chloe Cannell writes short stories for teens and adults; her characters are often queer and anxious like her. She is completing a queer short story cycle as part of her creative writing PhD at the University of South Australia. Her research project investigates intersectional LGBTQIA+ representations in contemporary young adult fiction and writing workshops as a method of writing in allyship. Chloe is a fan of many things including musicals, cabaret, sitcoms, comedy podcasts, and the many forms of cooked potatoes. Keep up with Chloe on her Instagram @chloejcannell.

Author Statement

My first thought on the green prompt was the lawn out the front of my rental that I hated maintaining. I could argue lawns are bad for the environment but really I'm just not an outside person. The beauty of this anthology's theme is how we played with green in various ways.

'Emerald or Teal Green?' is inspired by the few times I've been to weddings and noticed the different kinds of love, hope and sometimes conflict that emerge at those celebrations. Green is envy for the life the protagonist Makala wants: nice dresses, a fancy wedding, and a typical loving family. When Makala's past jeopardises the future she hopes for, how will she respond?

My micro story 'Invasive Species' is in response to another story that was one of the original submissions to this anthology, 'Seventy Two' by Aden Burg. I usually stay in my comfort zone of realism so it was a fun experiment to write from a non-human perspective in a fantasy world. The opposite of green is humans killing the environment for their own gain. Another writer in this anthology, Dante DeBono, gave me the title for this story.

Dante DeBono

Author Bio

Dante is an Adelaide-based creative with a life-long passion for artistry. In recent times, her focus has been on honing her skills as a writer, having graduated from a Bachelor of Journalism and Professional Writing, a Bachelor of Arts (English and Creative Writing), and receiving a First Class Honours Degree. Currently, she is a PhD candidate at the University of South Australia with the goal of promoting social inclusivity and equality through work focussed on diversifying queer representation in research and creative outputs. Dante's work can be followed on Instagram at @ dante_debono.

Author Statement

When tasked with the prompt of 'green' for this anthology, I found most of my inspiration in nature—something of a constant in my life. I've always felt very connected to our environment and while not all of my pieces deal with plant life directly, there is an undercurrent of the natural world that runs throughout. Knowing that I would have much to say about green things, I chose to engage with short form writing, primarily poetry which has a long history of utilising nature as muse and metaphor. At first, I was surprised by how personal 'green' felt to me but have come to realise that the introspective element was what I needed to feel satisfied by my work. Threads of truth are generally the catalysts for my writing, and this anthology gave me the chance to unpack both passing notions from my life, as well as larger concerns that have only been exacerbated by the difficulty of the last few years. As a result, I like to think my pieces encourage a similar types of contemplation: some for yourself, some for others, some for a bigger picture, and some for the Earth as a whole. I can only hope that any resulting thoughts from the reader are empathetic and understanding, even if it's only for the weeds that peek through cracks in footpaths.

Lyndal Hordacre Kobayashi

Author Bio

Lyndal Hordacre Kobayashi loves experimenting with all things colourful and creative, whether it's her PhD journey in the Research Centre for Languages and Cultures, her mud-brick house, gardening, playing the violin, knitting, or creative writing. She has lived and worked as a visual artist, with 15 years in Europe and Japan, and is now using her background in the arts to encourage monolingual research participants to explore their lived experiences with language(s). Lyndal hopes to demonstrate the potential and relevance of heralding new knowledge by stepping into a sphere of creative activity, mystery, and discovery.

Lyndal has been interested in language and visual, critical, and creative forms of connecting for all of her professional life. She was fortunate enough to be selected to enter the National Academies of Fine Art in both Oslo and Vienna and has performed, danced, and exhibited in Europe, Japan, and Australia. She now lives in the Adelaide Hills, writing her PhD, working as a transpersonal art therapist, and caring for her youngest daughter with Down Syndrome. She speaks English, Norwegian and Japanese.

Lyndal has presented her creative work at the *Drawing International Symposium* in Brisbane, Queensland in 2015 and the *Australiasian Association of Writing Programs* in 2020. She has also contributed to the 2021 article, 'Reimagining the reading group: critically creative connectivity, care and resilience in academic cultures of challenge and change' and has her Master of Philosophy research, 'Researching the mindsets of monolinguals: a "linguistic self" of twenty-

first century monolingual art students in Australia' (2017)
published online.

Author Statement

Writing has been present throughout my travels and explorations, but never fully honed or explored until my university studies. Participation in the Critically Creative Reading and Writing Collective has given me the opportunity to draw confidently, holistically, critically, and creatively from the total of my lived experiences.

Participation in this anthology took me by surprise. I was totally obsessing over the need for visual images and explanations of creative processes in the volume and felt lost and desolate that I was the only visual artist aboard. I, therefore, decided to conjure up a vision and try to use words rather than pastels as creative tools, to carefully depict a vision being created, a story being told. It wasn't easy, but through this experience, I have taken a juicy bite out of a very delicious and satiating discovery.

Evan Jarrett

Author Bio

Evan Jarrett is an Honours Candidate in Creative Writing at the University of South Australia. His work explores how fictional world-making can communicate the complex intersections between climate change, class, and the multiplicity of place.

Evan was born in Adelaide, South Australia, and has long been fascinated with how places impact him, physically, emotionally, and, on a deeper level, spiritually. Growing up in a working-class suburb, he often reflects on how people both shape and are shaped by the places they interact with. He frequently wonders, with the multitudes of ways in which climate change is impacting on places across the world, how people from different backgrounds and in different situations will be shaped by climate change themselves, and how they may respond to this.

Author Statement

'Green Bay' is a short story about one man's experiences with a place and how it impacted him. It is a story about the vibrancy and interrelatedness of life, and how one's experiences with places can have profound, life-changing ramifications. It is about how a place can be both beautiful and welcoming, yet hostile and dangerous. Ultimately, it is about how a place can speak to you, and teach you—even call out for help, if you watch, listen, and experience what it has to offer. This story is in no way about myself. I cannot surf. I caught a wave on a bodyboard once and it was exhilarating.

What I remember most about it was the power of the ocean.
It made me feel so insignificant, and somehow, that was lib-
erating. I also remember the beach, and the trek out to the
beach. I remember the sights and the smells. I remember the
birds. 'Green Bay' highlights, overall, how the experiences
of places shape us. After all, had I never caught that wave, I
likely never would have written this piece.

Belinda Lees

Author Bio

Belinda Lees is a PhD candidate researching screenwriting under the supervision of Prof Craig Batty and Dr Amelia Walker through the University of South Australia. She previously completed an MA in screenwriting at Cornwall's Falmouth University.

Since then, she has had short films and a feature titled *The Clearing* produced by John Finnegan's screenwriting podcast *The Script Department*. Belinda has contributed around twenty comic children's plays to Australia's leading children's literary magazine *The School Magazine*. She is a past winner of the Todhunter Literary Award, which she won for a one-act absurdist play.

She works as an educator in a secondary school, teaching media and literature to senior students, where she draws on her credentials in performing arts, literature, media, and screenwriting.

Author Statement

'If Only Fences Kept Us Apart' looks at the complexity of personal environmental obligations when butting up against the challenges of interpersonal conflict. The questions explored in this story are: what do you do when someone else is compromising others' environmental integrity, what impact does this have on their sanity, and when does idealism become obsession? Sometimes, being 'green' is not as simple as doing one's part and minding one's business because people are messy and constantly transgress boundaries or 'fences'.

Comedy is often my style of choice, especially with shorter pieces, as I find I can pack more punch by making people laugh. Comedy provides distance but also an opportunity for identification. For this piece, I was inspired by a neighbour who drove me to distraction and immense frustration over a period of six years, until she and her massive tribe finally moved out. In nearly every way imaginable, her life spilled over into mine, including her constant sneaking of trash into my bins. While the protagonist is not based on me, I think we all have a little bit of Celia in us, perhaps a little bit more than we care to admit. As we see through Celia, it can be difficult to maintain balance when someone else is compromising our idealistic values. Question: what do you do? Answer: turn it into a short story.

Heather Briony McGinn

Author Bio

Heather Briony McGinn is a PhD candidate at the University of South Australia with a research focus on Beat Studies and feminist literary criticism. In the first year of her postgraduate research she developed *l'écriture kinesthésique*, a corporeal-based creative writing methodology.

Author Statement

I have developed kinaesthetic writing, or *l'écriture kinesthésique*, in order to marry kinesis to the corporeal. A kinaesthetic approach to writing calls for vulnerable and feminist practice that amplifies previously silenced or untold narratives. Guided by Beat Studies, my practice is experimental, incorporates cut-ups and bricolage, and is often written while performing the role of *flâneuse* (Castaleo-Gomez 2016, p. 58).

Australian writer and academic Dallas J Baker asserts that '...writing practice and engagement with textual artefacts (literature) can trigger and inform queer self-making.' (2011, p. 39).

I have chosen the queer deviant body and the text it produces as the site of my research.

Why?

The answer is simple: Firstly, my body is an incorrect one, and secondly, I am a poet. I cannot separate my existence from text. I understand everything through the kaleidoscopic lens of poetry processed through a neurodivergent brain and a chronically ill corpus. The text produced by my body is shot through with eroticism, kink, pain, and taboo, making it unsettling, ugly, and exposing.

The tool I use to release this text from my body is kinaesthetic writing, a technique that explores embodied text and vulnerabilities and extends Hélène Cixous' theory of *écriture feminine* (1976, p. 875) and declared by Cixous herself to be 'The language that women speak when no one is there to correct them' (1991, p. 21). A kinaesthetic approach to writing calls for vulnerable and feminist practice that amplifies previously silenced or untold narratives. Eades' assertion that the body is a site of resistance that is always already text (2015, p. 30) has galvanised me to the task of working within a theory that allows the body to speak to the disruption of queering practice. The resistance to normative forms that is fostered by *écriture kinesthétique* creates text that is steeped in otherness and prone to hybridity.

'Kinaesthetic writing has the ability to disrupt, to fracture, to witness, and to reckon with the unspeakable...' (McGinn 2019). It is ideal for those researching through the Queered PLR model, as well as an effective tool for the unearthing rhizomatic and/or feminist narratives.

Lily Roberts

Author Bio

Lily May Roberts (she/her) is a Bachelor of Creative Arts (Honours) student at UniSA focusing on auto-ethnographic poetic practice. She was born and raised in Adelaide and her work concentrates on recovery from trauma and addiction through an engagement with the sensory and the spiritual. Lily is especially interested in exploring how poetry crosses over with mindfulness, the phenomenology of the embodied poet, and the development of an ecological method of relating that encourages systems-thinking for situating the self. Further down the track, she is interested in cultivating her own poetry therapy approach for recovering addicts and sexual assault survivors.

Lily was awarded the Cecil Teesdale Smith Literary Award in 2021.

Author Statement

In responding to the prompt 'Green', I was taken back to my childhood, when I took ballet classes at the Mitcham Institute. Inside one of the halls was a folding mirror that I was small enough to climb inside, and once I was in there, it became an infinity mirror, a sonorous visual echo of my own little frame and face repeating back to me endlessly. Mirrors are made from commercial glass, which means they have a green tint to them—you'll find iron and other impurities in the glass that lend it that colour. It's why some glasshouses and older art deco buildings look the way they do. That deepening green in the infinity mirror is a meditation on memory and its cascading iterations, and unfolds like a poem might… My poems start at arbitrary points and can be read as flowing on from one another in an infinite stream of consciousness, attempting to contain a dialectic between the concrete and the intangible. I interacted closely with the natural world of my garden in order to write the poems that I contributed. The slow death of my father unfolded alongside the creation of this anthology, which led to the inclusion of meditations on young life, and life during and after death.

Eugene Tabios

Author Bio

It was during his high school years when Eugene Tabios had been first lured in by the wonder of the minutiae, discovering and eventually submitting flash fiction to *Sobrang Short Stories*. In 2016, his 100-word story, 'Christmas Eve', won fourth place and his later, even shorter piece, 'The Fateful Day', written under his penname Placido Penitorpe, received publication in *The Best of Sobrang Short Stories*.

When he moved from the Philippines to Australia, Eugene decided to pursue a career in humanities, a stark contrast to his initial plan to be an accountant. Since then, he has dedicated himself to discovering new things, studying their intricacies, embracing their fleetingness, and putting them in writing, guided by his self-coined mantra to 'observe and preserve'.

Eugene is an emerging writer currently undertaking his Bachelor's degree in Creative Writing and Linguistics at the University of South Australia.

Author Statement

Japanese, African, and Southeast Asian folklore speak of what is commonly called a 'fox's wedding', an otherworldly phenomenon of ghostly lights forming, as if in a procession, during the instance of a sunshower.

Marriages signify a sort of 'death' of the individual, which may be why some see this event as an omen of danger or misfortune. By committing oneself to wedlock, you relinquish a life that you have lived in adherence to yourself and yourself alone.

Of course, there is a duality to this: other beliefs surrounding the fox's wedding imply a bountiful year of harvest. A time to amass new chances and new experiences. Rain washes over regrets of the past and begins life anew.

Our lives are inevitably tied to nature, through meetings and goodbyes, through life and death, through ends and beginnings. 'Of Simpler Times' is my tribute to the ephemeral that, whilst brief and fleeting, will always signify tomorrow.

Simon-Peter Telford

Author Bio

Simon-Peter is a writer and poet from South Australia. He is a PhD candidate and teaches Creative Writing at the University of South Australia, where his research involves writing existential fiction for the Anthropocene.

Author Statement

Working with the writers of this anthology over the past few years has been a rewarding and stimulating experience, and working with Dr Alex Dunkin and Buon-Cattivi Press to develop this anthology was a wonderful experience. They are not only formidable colleagues but cherished friends.

Writing 'What if I Called You Wally?' was an intense process of reflection and a challenging project in narrative. I set out to write a story on loss and the aging process, of those in our society we have deemed expendable. Vin has lived many lives and is filled with stories, yet he has no one to sit with and share a cup of tea or glass of port. A twist on Ahab and his white whale, perhaps, Vin sees his own existence and worth in Wally, and as much as his goal was to comfort the dying creature, it was a comfort for him to feel alive once more, for it is often only in having others witness our life, do we feel alive. As I often think, nature and animals can become a mirror for our own existence. Our most human moments can come from our interactions with the non-human.

Telling a compelling story that is essentially a one-way dialogue was difficult at times. It pushed me as a writer to think about the craft, when to put in some action, when a little groan from poor old Wally helped break up Vin's story. It is my hope that readers experience the sweet sadness of this story and, if still possible, reach out to those who may need to tell a tale or relive a memory.

Works Cited

Baker, D 2011, 'Queering Practice-Led Research: Subjectivity, performative research and the creative arts', *Creative Industries Journal*, vol. 4, no. 1, pp. 33-51.

Castelao-Gomez, I 2016, 'Beat Women Poets and Writers: Countercultural Urban Geographies and Feminist Avant-Garde Politics', *Journal of English Studies*, vol. 14, pp. 47-72.

Cixous, H, Cohen, K, and Cohen, P 1976, 'The Laugh of the Medusa', *Journal of Women in Culture and Society*, vol 1, no 4, pp. 875-893.

Eades, Q 2015, 'all the beginnings', *Tantanoola/Australian Scholarly Publishing Ltd.*, North Melbourne, Victoria, Australia.

McGinn, HB 2019, 'Writing through the disobedient body: how body poetics can be a place from which queer women's narratives can rise and be heard', *presentation at Australasian Association of Writing Programs (AAWP) Annual Conference*, University of Technology Sydney, 27 November 2019.

McGinn, HB 2017, 'Writing the (raped) body, Art(i)culations of Violence, *Writing from Below*, vol. 3, no. 2, section 2, La Trobe University, Melbourne, Australia.

Merleau-Ponty, M 1974, *Phenomenology of Perception*, trans C Smith, Aylesbury: Compton Printing Limited.

9 781922 314079